A TEACUP FULL OF ROSES

Joe had a brother who painted like a god—when he wasn't
too busy pumping drugs into his arm. Joe himself had a
gift. He could tell stories that made people laugh or cry—
or believe what they needed to believe. He had promised
Ellie that when they were married they would live in a
magical place where trouble never came: "in a teacup . . .
full of roses." For two long years Joe worked full-time and
sweated out night school for the diploma that was supposed to open the doors to college and heaven itself. Then
something happened that changed all their lives. It cost Joe
what he loved most, robbed him of his final hope, but per-
haps it brought him his soul.

Also by Sharon Bell Mathis

Sidewalk Story
Listen for the Fig Tree
The Hundred Penny Box

TEACUP
FULL OF ROSES

SHARON BELL MATHIS

PUFFIN BOOKS

PUFFIN BOOKS
Published by the Penguin Group
Penguin Young Readers Group,
345 Hudson Street, New York, New York 10014, U.S.A.
Penguin Group (Canada), 90 Eglinton Avenue East, Suite 700, Toronto,
Ontario, Canada M4P 2Y3 (a division of Pearson Penguin Canada Inc.)
Penguin Books Ltd, 80 Strand, London WC2R 0RL, England
Penguin Ireland, 25 St Stephen's Green, Dublin 2, Ireland
(a division of Penguin Books Ltd)
Penguin Group (Australia), 250 Camberwell Road, Camberwell, Victoria 3124,
Australia (a division of Pearson Australia Group Pty Ltd)
Penguin Books India Pvt Ltd, 11 Community Centre, Panchsheel Park,
New Delhi - 110 017, India
Penguin Group (NZ), 67 Apollo Drive, Mairangi Bay, Auckland 1311,
New Zealand (a division of Pearson New Zealand Ltd)
Penguin Books (South Africa) (Pty) Ltd, 24 Sturdee Avenue,
Rosebank, Johannesburg 2196, South Africa

Registered Offices: Penguin Books Ltd, 80 Strand, London WC2R 0RL, England

First published in the United States of America by The Viking Press, 1972
Published by Puffin Books, 1987
Reissued by Puffin Books, a division of Penguin Young Readers Group, 2007

27 28 29 30

Copyright © Sharon Bell Mathis, 1972
All rights reserved

Acknowledgment
William Morrow & Company, Inc.: from *Black Feeling, Black Talk, Black Judgment* by
Nikki Giovanni, copyright © 1968, 1970 by Nikki Giovanni. Reprinted by permission.
Set in Times Roman

Library of Congress catalog card number: 86-42986
(CIP data available)

Puffin Books ISBN 978-0-14-032328-3

Printed in the United States of America

For my husband.
And my brother. But
especially for my father
JOHN "RED" BELL
who stood me up on game tables
when I was a baby
and told me I brought him luck
and
some good numbers

And for my little black friend
VIDA LYNN ROUSELLE
who said she wanted her name in a book

Teacup Full of Roses

"i wanta say just gotta say something bout those beautiful beautiful beautiful outasight black men . . ."

—Nikki Giovanni
Black Feeling, Black Talk, Black Judgment

1

"Sorry, Pop," Joe said, "I got something to do."

"Listen, Joseph. Please, son, I'm asking you please stay here. Your mother's going to come in here and be upset and blaming me if this dinner tonight for your brother Paul don't turn out right for her." The thin-faced man, sitting on the dining-room chair in an over-sized, faded blue bathrobe, glanced at his wife's picture on the buffet. "I ain't ever seen Mattie look happy as she look last night when that boy come home. She ain't smiled the whole seven months he been away. She couldn't sleep last night for worrying about this dinner and us showing Paul we behind him in this thing." The man's lips were trembling and he looked older than he was. With what seemed a mighty effort, he gained control of himself and stopped shaking. "I kept my eye on him soon as he and you and Mattie hit that door. But I can't tell nothing yet. Maybe that hospital cleaned him off that stuff for good, I don't know. But it didn't seem right to me, him not being here all day. Came in late last night and gone already, soon's your mother left for work. Doing just like he used to." The man wheezed, his breath coming suddenly short. "That's why I called you at work, so you can look for him and see what's going on. But you come in here telling me you got something else to do."

Joe looked at his father. Looked at the robe he wore, left over from his "over 200 pounds" days, when he wasn't sick. Just strong and quiet. But now the carefully ironed faded robe seemed to wrap the thin body like some washed-out, still protective thing holding on gently to what was left of the man.

The boy looked away.

"Your mother's all keyed up over tonight and I'll be the blame when things go wrong."

Joe walked to the hall closet, got the shoebox, and came back and sat down in the chair nearest his father. "You're great, Pop," he said. "You not the blame for nothing, 'less it's something good. If I see Paul while I'm out—I'll try to get him home. But I got to go see a man now. It's important." Joe picked a clean rag from the crowded box and began to snap it back and forth across his expensive-looking shoes. "Otherwise, I'd do what you want. You know that."

Isaac Brooks leaned closer to his son. "Your brother's back there studying," he said quietly. "How come you don't have nothing to study, you graduating Thursday?

Seems to me you ought to be doing *some* kind of studying."

"Don't need it, Pop. Neither does Davey. Davey's got it made even if he never opens another book. I think he's read them all anyway. Thursday, all they got to do is give me the piece of paper I been working for. And that's it." The boy kept up a steady rhythm with the snapping rag.

"Listen, Joseph. Stop messing with them shoes . . . listen to me!" The boy stopped. But when he put down the rag, the father looked uncomfortable. "Now, well, go on . . . go on and finish what you doing."

Joe started snapping the cloth again.

"All I'm asking is, get Paul in here, then go on to your class and get back here and eat. So your mother can be happy. What you got to do maybe can wait till tomorrow."

No, Joe thought, it can't wait.

"I'm begging you, Joseph, son. I don't know what else I can do."

"You do the best you can, Pop," Joe said gently.

The father dropped his head and stared at the floor. For a while he sat still. Then suddenly he got up and looked hard at the clock. "Look," he said. But then he sat down again and watched silently while Joe finished shining his shoes.

Joe looked carefully at his shoes before he folded the rag, put it neatly back inside the wooden box, and placed the whole thing back in the hall closet. "Maybe you could

11

knock Momma down, Pop," he said. "Knock her down if she comes through that door wrong. Maybe you're too gentle and she can't use it."

It was hard to tell whether it was what the boy said or how he said it that brought the stricken look to the man's face. "I never struck your mother," he said finally in a low voice. "And I never will. She's got enough trouble. A man don't need to strike a woman and don't you ever do it."

"Maybe it would prove something, Pop," Joe said in a voice as quiet as his father's.

"Joseph, how you going to stand there and tell me hit your mother. You'd kill somebody if they *looked* at your mother wrong."

"You got that right."

"Then why you talking like this?"

"Just talk, Pop. Just talk." Joe walked across the dining room to the buffet mirror, pulled an African pic from his pocket, and started combing his well-shaped Afro. After a moment, he checked the roundness and reshaped a few places. "Talking don't mean nothing," he said, "and I know it." Joe stepped back from the mirror. "I been talking at night school two years and maybe that don't mean nothing either. On Thursday, the talk ends—it'll be over. And I'll be—"

"Oooooooooooooh, Lord Jesus! Oooooooooh!"

The sound came from a small woman seated on an upholstered window bench framed by three windows.

Her hair looked like it should have whitened years ago, but hadn't. The black dress, left over from bygone days, was too big for her, but she washed it each night and wore it every day. She sat on the window seat every day too, fingering the small leather pouch she never let out of her sight. Her skin was stretched taut as rubber over her bones and showed no signs of age. Only her hands did. Large, knotted, and wrinkled, with no softness in them, they told the story of a long, hard struggle.

Joe looked in the dining-room alcove. "Take it easy, Aunt Lou," he said. "Everything's all right, you just take it easy."

The piercing scream came again.

But this time, Joe ignored the sound. "Tell everybody, Aunt Lou. I got it made when Thursday comes."

"Oooooh, Jesus, have mercy! Have mercy, Jesus!"

Isaac Brooks turned to the bony frame of his oldest sister. The moaning continued. "Ummmmm, Lord Jesus. Ummmmmmm!"

"Llouvah! Stop that noise. You going to make Joseph leave. Hush!"

"Nobody's making me leave, Pop. Especially Aunt Lou." The boy walked into the tiny alcove and hugged the old woman. "Aunt Lou," he said, "you know everything. You know I got to go out. Tell Pop. Tell him I got something to do." He kissed her forehead.

She was staring at him. "Joseph Matthew," she whispered.

"Tell Pop about Davey too, Aunt Lou, while you at it. Tell him Davey doesn't need to do no studying. He makes the only *A*'s in the whole school. In fact, they'd close the joint if it wasn't for Davey."

"Joseph Matthew," she whispered again.

"What about Davey's long legs and that outasight basketball arm he got. Davey going to play great ball, you and I know that. Tell Pop—so he'll know too."

"Spirits speaking to me, Joseph Matthew. Bad this time, my bones feel trouble. If I open this bag, I see it. But I ain't got to open it. I ain't got to see it to know it bad, Joseph Matthew. Spirits never wrong. Didn't I tell you when Maceo die? Ain't I knew 'bout Cora's child? Ain't wrong this time either." The moan that came then was low-sounding and long.

"Llouvah! I told you now. Damn it, hush!" The man got up quickly but sat right back down. He was looking at the clock. He looked at Joe. "Listen, Joseph, your mother asked me to get some fish for dinner but she didn't leave no money. You got some change? Thought I had some but I don't." He was looking at the clock again.

Joe took his wallet out, handed his father ten dollars, and put his wallet away. But he took it out again and put another bill in his father's hand. "For you," he said.

"I got money," his father said quietly and put the money in his bathrobe pocket. "But your mother's got it in the bank, saving it for a house, and she don't want nobody touching it. Couldn't leave no money laying

14

'round Paul no way. Though maybe it'd be safe now with him off that junk."

This time it was Joe who looked at the clock. I got time, he thought, and took his freshly ironed shirt from the back of a chair. From the window seat in the alcove, Joe could hear his name being chanted softly over and over.

"Your mother didn't say what fish she wants for tonight. Paul'll eat any kind of fish period, but she'll be fussing and carrying on if I don't get what she wants."

Joe stopped buttoning his shirt. "Davey can do it," he said.

"Okay, David can get the fish. But you go take care your business, then try to find Paul and get him back here. You said you leaving your classes early tonight anyway to be back here for this dinner. So you can go late too, just this once for me. You not changing your mind about being here tonight? You not doing that?"

"No, Pop."

"Good. Everything's got to go like Mattie planned it. The right fish. Paul here. Everything."

"Tell you what," Joe said. "Have Paul at the door when Momma comes. Let her see him first and she'll be so busy smiling she won't care whether you got fish or dog food. Stick one of his artist's brushes in his hand." Joe was silent for a moment and when he spoke, his voice was too soft. "And Momma won't care who else in the family is in or out."

15

But the father hadn't noticed his son's voice. "You think Paul's going to remember this dinner?" he asked, lips slightly quivering. "Your mother talked about it enough, but Paul was fooling around, teasing."

"He'll remember."

"What's he got to stay out all day like this for? Away seven months. He comes back and poof! He's gone again, like a ghost. I hope he ain't dying. I'm hoping as much for Mattie's sake as his."

"He may make it this time. I think that OD scared him. What you think, Aunt Lou?" Joe had asked her this question for seven months and she had never answered.

She didn't answer now. She wasn't even moving now. Though her eyes were open there seemed to be no life in her. It was as if the most minute functions of her body had quietly ceased.

Both father and son stared at her.

"HEY, JOEY! Where's my green shirt?" a voice yelled in falsetto.

"Hey, Joey! Where's my green shirt?" Joe yelled back, mimicking his brother and glad for the distraction from the unnaturally still woman.

"Aww, Joey, man. My voice can't sound that bad! You wear my green shirt?"

"Davey, baby. That's *not* my kind of material, man." Joe walked down the hallway to the back bedroom he shared with his brothers. He heard his father saying, "Llouvah! You don't have to sit like that. Llouvah!"

Joe did a quick step to his youngest and tallest brother

and a couple more quick steps and landed a heavy punch to the boy's stomach. "Watch your belly," he said. "Your green shirt's on the roof, line near the door."

David stooped and tied the laces of his tennis shoes.

"Forget the green shirt, put on your sweats, and get on the court and throw some. After that, Pop needs you to get fish for tonight."

"I can get the fish but I already practiced. It went pretty good."

"Like perfect?"

"It was okay."

"So where you heading?"

"Library."

"Davey, man, there's no books left you haven't read, man. You must got something else going for you at the library." Joe kept his face straight and watched his brother trying to figure out whether he was serious.

"Heck, no, Joey. Not girls. Girls don't even know how to talk to you, man."

"Tell me you kidding, baby."

"All they say is 'Hey, David. Can I ask you something?' Then when I stop and say what, all they do is stand there laughing and bumping into each other. The longer I stand there waiting, the more they laugh and fall all over the sidewalk. And when I walk away one of them yells something dumb like, 'HEY, DAVID BROOKS. HOW TALL ARE YOU?' or 'Tell Joe I said hello.' "

"Know what?" Joe said.

"What?"

"Man, I really believe you and me can't talk women yet. You not ready! Only thing I believe it's time for is you just going up and getting your green shirt."

"Uh, yeah." David jumped up and almost through the door in one long stride. "Hope Momma hung it up right, so I don't have to iron it."

"*Hold up, Davey.* Just hold it, man. I got to tell you something. You listening?"

"Yeah, but hurry up."

"You saying some wrong things."

"What wrong things?"

"Like not ironing shirts, Davey, baby. That's not the way, man. What you got to do is iron the shirt and step in that library looking pretty, so you don't blow something good. You know what I mean?"

David waited.

"I got a story for you."

"I've got to go, man!" David's voice cracked a bit.

"Hold it. This is just a little story. It's about a cool dude, didn't know how cool he was. Fact is, he was the dumbest smart guy you ever saw. So one day something happened. In a library is where it happened, man!"

David was on his way through the door again.

"Hold it, see. You said you'd listen. What I was saying is the prettiest black girl in the world is in that library, man. And not only is she pretty, she's smart too. But nobody in the library can help her find what she has to find, except this dude in the wrinkled green shirt. And the situation don't look good, see. 'Cause after he helps

18

her, she forgets him. All she remembers is the wrinkled shirt. And I don't think it's so good when a fine chick thinks you not together. Especially when you really are."

Joe, watching his brother's handsome dark face, knew his story had worked. Since David was a baby—he was fifteen now—Joe had made up stories for him. Thinking about it and looking at the scratched beige alarm clock, broken and fixed by each of the three brothers, Joe suddenly felt older than seventeen.

David saw him staring at the clock. "I heard you and Pop out there," he said. "Where you going?"

"Warwick," Joe said.

David flinched, then seemed to go into a stupor. "No, Joey," he managed to say, "don't go, Joey. Don't mess with Warwick. Paul's all right now, he's out." Behind his eyeglasses David's eyes were staring, and his panic made his voice tight. "Warwick'll kill you. He'd kill anybody. He'll *kill* you, Joey!"

"It won't come easy for him," Joe said on his way out of the room. But he stopped when he saw the easel, Paul's easel, braced against a makeshift fluorescent light. Joe looked at the heavy buff-colored paper held to the easel with masking tape. The penciled sketch of a black infant boy with a prophet's eyes looked back at him. "When Paul do this?" Joe asked. But David was still staring at his brother. "When?" Joe asked again.

"Early this morning. But he stopped after Momma left."

Joe turned on the fluorescent light and saw that the

19

baby's fantastically lifelike eyes looked like Paul's. He turned the light off. "Maybe I can talk to Warwick," he said.

"I'm going with you," David announced, no longer stiff.

Joe snapped around so fast David flinched. "You stick to the ball and the books," he said, grabbing a light-tan jacket from the closet. "You don't know the street yet."

"I thought you would stay like I asked you," his father said when he saw Joe walking to the front door.

"No, Pop."

"Joseph Matthew, trouble coming! Trouble coming hard to this house." Aunt Lou was no longer still. Her eyes seemed oddly bright, almost luminous.

"I think it's here already, Aunt Lou," Joe said. "I think trouble lives in this house." His voice was soft, for a moment, like his father's. "I don't have no little black bag to look in, but I know."

His aunt's moaning and his father's "Hush!" were the last things Joe heard as he walked down four flights of steps to the street. The elevator, fixed each month, was out of order again.

But outside, the street didn't need fixing. It was wonderful, Joe thought. He could almost forget the things that worried him. But not quite.

Like where was Paul?

And his plan to talk to Warwick. Would it go right? Why hadn't he thought of it while Paul was away?

20

2

"Joe! Hey, Joe. Wait!"

"No time for a story today, Willie." Willie, Joe thought quickly, still on crutches and still smiling. The little boy who'd proved you could get hit by a dump truck and live.

"Just a teensy-weensy one? Real, real, *real* short!"

Joe wondered how anybody could get around Willie's great black African eyes. Maybe that's why the dump truck hadn't finished him off. How could anybody destroy eyes that beautiful? The more Willie talked, the larger they got. Joe planned to really test them out one day. But not now.

"And don't tell me no stories about big trucks that talk about kids playing in the street, because trucks can't talk!"

"Say what!" Joe teased him.

"You said you was going to tell me a black story."

"Okay, little chump. Next time I'll tell you about a

black dude named Hannibal. He was a great general that had his army riding elephants like the elephants were tanks, man. Then, one day they had some water to cross —see. So my story is how he made it across. Okay?"

"You going to tell me on your way back? Promise?"

Joe laughed. "You know how to hustle somebody don't you! Okay, tell you what, you catch me coming back and I'll tell you about Hannibal. I promise." Joe watched Willie run back to the stoop. Running fast on crutches, with one foot missing. Yeah, little Hannibal, Joe thought, I promise.

A clock in a cleaner's window read 5:18. The tip on Warwick was that he wasn't going to be at the record shop until after five thirty. I've got time, Joe thought. And maybe the right information.

It wasn't easy to track Warwick. He could flick away fast. Joe thought of the pusher's tiny birdlike feet, slim, prancing ankles, and childlike shoulders. Joe remembered the drawing he had held in his hands a few minutes ago. Hold on, Paul, he thought. Warwick don't have to be your bag no more. It's you and me.

"Man! Nothing you thinking can make you look bad as you do now."

Phil's voice. Phil, his friend, was beside him, just like always in trouble time. A scene slipped into Joe's mind— he and Phil together once before.

"You bleeding, man!"

"Cool it, Phil, I'm all right. Ace cut me. You see Ace? I can't see too good."

22

"*Ace by the window.*"

"*Cover me!*"

"THE COPS! *Oh, hell, man, Ace cut you bad. Hold on to me. Yeah, that's it. We getting out this damn store!*"

"*I said cover me.*"

"*Forget it, man! We get Ace later. Right now, I got to climb this fire escape for both our behinds.* JOE! ACE IN BACK OF US! WHAT YOU WANT TO DO?"

"*Slow down when we get to the fire escape.*"

Phil, with a voice deep as bedrock and a fist as hard. He had lived in nine foster homes before he found a family that loved him. He could strum an electric guitar and sing better than anyone on records.

"What's happening?"

"Nothing," Joe said.

"Something's always happening, baby. Let's go find it."

"Later, Phil."

"Cool."

"Where you walking, Phil?" Joe said.

"I'm walking where you walking."

"I can't use you right now."

"Oh, man, Ellie's!" Phil said and did a little bougaloo step on the sidewalk.

"I'm not going over Ellie's. I'm going over Warwick's."

"Warwick's!"

"I'm going to talk."

"How you figuring, man? What's wrong with you?"

"Nothing. I'm going to see if I can work a deal about Paul. Unless it's too late and Paul got to him already."

23

"Warwick won't give you the time of day."

"Warwick understands money."

"You ain't got enough money to rap with Warwick."

"His own brother was killed on a dope double cross. Maybe he can dig how I feel."

"Warwick don't care 'bout your *mother!* Know what he brags about?"

"What?" Joe was interested. It might help to know.

"How bad his stuff is. Says you can die faster using his."

Joe felt suddenly like gutting somebody hard, gutting them bad. "Shut up, Phil," he said.

"Warwick don't help nobody but Warwick. He's a mean dude, like maybe his mother and father didn't know each other. Like maybe they just walked past each other and Warwick happened. He ain't real."

"I said shut up."

"If you going, I'm going."

Joe only had a few more blocks to go. K Street and Warwick were minutes away. "I don't need you, Phil."

"You don't know that yet."

"Don't be begging for trouble. You got it made now, people caring for you. Don't mess up. If I need you another time—maybe you'll be there. Like old times. You and me busting heads."

"All you got to do is say the word."

"Yeah, I know it, Phil."

The two boys looked at each other for a moment, embarrassed, then grinned and moved along again. Phil's face, as Joe walked away, seemed to say, You can't beat this thing with Paul and Warwick. Joe's eyes agreed but added, Maybe.

Joe saw them first. Eight of them. There were always eight of them; people said Warwick liked the number eight. Nobody knew why.

Joe walked toward the young hoodlums unafraid. Davey had the rep for basketball, but Joe had it for street fighting. He hadn't been warlord of the Royals for nothing, and he knew that even though his last fight had been two years ago, he hadn't forgotten how. When he needed that kind of strength again, it would come.

The eight boys weren't afraid either. Joe was only one.

"Warwick," Joe said. "Where can I find him?"

"Man, we don't know nobody name Warwick."

"Don't be silly, you guys," said one of the boys, imitating a woman's voice. "What you want to treat Brooks like that for? Ain't Warwick the name that guy was swinging up on those trees a few minutes ago?" The boy giggled. "You know. Like Tarzan!" He giggled again. "My main monkey!"

"I got to see Warwick. It's important."

"He just fell out the sky, man."

"Yeah." They started laughing hard.

"Wait it, people—maybe we can help Brooks. But we got to do it scientific. The word 'war' mean fight. Ain't that right?"

"Right," they all agreed.

25

"And ain't a wick something you find stuck down the middle a candle? Ain't that yeah?"

"Yeah," they all said.

"Well then, what we looking for and talking 'bout is a fightin' candle!"

Joe walked away. He couldn't win now. The time was wrong for it. The boys were laughing hard and slapping hands. "But a candle can't walk," he heard one of them say.

"That don't mean it can't fight! What you know 'bout candles! You ain't no candle expert!"

"Man, you can't even spell 'expert'!"

As he reached the corner, one boy ran up and touched him. "Brooks, if you see a candle walking, we'll—" Joe hit him with a solid blow deep in the stomach. The punch was so hard and so sudden that the boy was too stunned to fall. His eyes stretched fully round. Joe grinned.

"You should have stayed with your friends. It's funky out here by yourself," Joe said, still grinning.

The other boys began to walk toward them. Joe looked at them and smiled. They started laughing then and stayed where they were.

The boy was getting his breath again. He started coughing. "The next time . . ." he managed to say.

Joe reached for the boy's hand and shook it before he could snatch it back. "I know," Joe said and pointed back to the boys. "I know, I know—but what I want you to do is walk back straight, making like you know how to take care yourself." Joe didn't stop smiling until he turned the corner.

Then he ran. Across streets and around more corners. He wasn't sure they had chased him—there had been no time to think about it.

There was no time now either. Paul was standing at the bus stop, waiting for him. Just like he used to do, to get money from Joe before he got on the bus on his way to night school.

Joe thought he looked all right. His eyes were open, he wasn't leaning. He wasn't in a nod.

But Joe walked over with a sharp eye.

"Little brother. Sugar. I been waiting for you," Paul said. Joe saw the bar of chocolate candy in his brother's hand.

"Are you straight, man?"

"Ease up, sugar." Paul took a bite of the candy. He was smiling. Not many people could resist his smile, and Joe, in spite of the feeling that was crawling along inside him, smiled too. "Want some?"

"No, man. I don't want no candy and I think you should cool it. Momma's planning a dinner to celebrate your being home. I'm leaving school early, so I can make it back."

"Little brother, my main man!"

"You going home, Paul?"

"I'm there already! Dave and Pop and Aunt Lou and you and me and Momma."

Joe didn't answer and Paul reached for him, and Joe

27

let him reach for him and hug him. The bony arms that folded about him made Joe feel like crying, only that wouldn't help this favorite son of Mattie Edwards Brooks. This oldest son, Joe knew, she loved above the rest of her children, this twenty-four-year-old gifted shell of a person who was his mother's dream of everything good in the world.

"You not straight, are you Paul?"

Paul released him. He was still smiling. "Hey, yeah, I'm okay. I had me a couple drinks with Bessie. You remember Bessie? That's where I been all day. Only left to get here to meet you. All the junk's out, I can't go back to it, man. It washed me out, dragged me, sucked me. Ruined me, man. You know that. I can't mess up no more. Pop and Aunt Lou wasn't even speaking to me. That's over now. I'm going to be somebody. I'm going to paint."

Joe felt a crawling thing snaking its way through his brain.

"Promised some of the doctors I'd do some paintings for them. But one of them told me which colors to use, so it could match his furniture. He only wanted the part of my soul that matched his furniture." Weak laughter came out.

Paul's bones, it seemed to Joe, were suspended in his clothes. Joe had hoped that Paul would gain weight while he was at the rehabilitation hospital. But if he had, it wasn't showing. At six feet one, Paul weighed less than a hundred and thirty pounds.

28

"I think they should get the painting first and *then* go buy the damn furniture!"

Joe leaned against the bus-stop pole.

"They told me about some art scholarships they'd help me get. But that never got around to happening."

Joe noticed Paul was wearing one of Davey's sweaters. It was way too large.

Paul touched his chest. "I got it in here," he murmured. "I don't have to wait for no scholarship to do nothing for me." He took another bite of candy. "You know that?"

"I know I want you to make it."

Paul shrugged what was left of his shoulders. "I'll make it."

"I don't think you want to."

"You wrong, little brother."

"You strung right now. The way you talking. You on that cloud doing it."

"No. No more. I been through hell at that place. And every day, somebody was asking me how I felt. It got so bad I didn't know which was worse. The hell I was going through—or them asking how it was!"

"What you getting ready to do now?"

"I'm going home and paint a portrait of Momma." Paul grinned then, but his grin faded. "She wants to dress up but that ain't what I want. What I want is to paint her in a shadow, only I can't figure what I want her in the shadow of. For years I been trying to figure it." Paul backed off a bit from Joe. "But I got the message for

29

you and me. I keep thinking about those stories you make up. You good, man. You can write the books and I do the pictures. We be a team, man! How about it, little brother, what you say?"

Joe saw the bus coming and part of him was relieved.

"You and me writing books. The first one will be about the toughest ball-playingest black dude there ever was. That part will be Dave. Ain't Dave great, man, ain't he great?"

"Yeah, Paul. Davey's great. You too."

"I used to watch him practice. But I'd stay outside the park and not go near him. Sometimes I didn't look too good and I didn't want him feeling shame." Paul's eyes brightened. "What you think about the book thing? You like it?"

The bus was there. "I like it," Joe said and touched his brother's arm. If he wanted, he could have encircled it with his fingers.

"We could do it, sugar. No sweat."

"You going home, Paul?"

"Right now, little brother. I'm going home right now." Paul dug in his loose pants pocket. "Take this," he said, handing Joe a Hershey. "I got two."

On the bus, Joe wondered. Was it too late to talk to Warwick? Had Paul messed up, or had he just had a few drinks, and maybe some reefers?

Later Joe sat in class thinking about Paul and knew he couldn't sit there any longer and got up and left. But he didn't feel like going home. You and Momma going to be out there by yourselves for a while, Paul, he thought. I just don't feel ready for it right now.

He called Ellie from a pay phone in the street, then took a bus to her house. To the drugstore across from her house, where he would meet her. But he sat there and remembered his mother's voice rather than Ellie's.

"Pray, Joe. Pray for your brother. He'll be home to-morrow. My baby's coming home and he's going to be all right. You should hear the doctors talking about the way he draws. I feel so proud. Paul makes me so proud."

Tonight Joe didn't feel the usual high he felt when he knew he would see Ellie.

What he felt was a low. A down trip.

3

Joe leaned against the drugstore window and stared up at Ellie's apartment. Lamplight, from within, made the fluffy curtains glow gently.

Those curtains are like her, he thought. Soft. And stupid-looking.

A small figure came to the window, peeked out, and waved. There was no need to wave back. It was their signal. She was coming out.

And she did. Trying to button her sweater and run at the same time. And grinning at him. A good grin, Joe thought, a nice one. Even with her teeth wired with the steel braces she hated. But most of all Ellie was one giant-sized bushy, virgin-wool-soft ponytail. Wet tree-bark color.

Once they had sat on a park retaining wall high above a winding highway and Joe had combed her hair into a huge Afro. Black people, driving along the highway, had raised fists in salute. Joe and Ellie had returned each one and smiled and felt good. But later on, the Afro had fallen, even though she had held her head as straight as she could. So Joe had combed it back into the ponytail and secured it with a scarf they had bought earlier that day in a bargain center.

Right then, watching Ellie, Joe decided not to smile back at her, to tease her, but he felt something good spreading through his body. It happened each time he saw her.

"Hi."

Joe said nothing.

"Look, Joe Brooks, there's no reason for you to look like that, because you haven't been out here that long! I kept going to the window right after you called, even when I knew you couldn't get here that fast. You couldn't have been out here more than a second before I looked out and saw you! I was doing my homework right *by* the window and . . ."

"Shut up, Ellie," Joe said and brushed his lips against her cheek. But when she turned her lips to him, he moved away.

"That's not a kiss, Joe!"

"How come you talk in exclamation points?"

"Because that's not a kiss, that's why!"

"It'll do. Let's go. What'd you tell your mother?"

"That I have to go to the library for something."

"You and Davey are real freaks for the library."

"It's as good a freak-out as any for a high school senior not allowed to have boy company in the house. Momma won't even let me talk to her about it. She just says 'plenty time'!"

"You get a chance to see your father last week?"

"No, Joe. He was busy."

"That bother you?"

"Naw, but it bothered my mother. She's never going to get over the divorce. She's always asking me what he's doing when I go over there and what his new wife is doing and what she's wearing and how they act with each other."

"And you say what?"

"I just say okay, I guess. I can't ever remember what she's wearing because she doesn't hang around Daddy and me when I'm there. So I can't hardly say what she's wearing."

"Good!"

"Good what?"

"Good, because your mother doesn't really want to know."

"Then how come she's always asking me stuff over and over? That doesn't sound like she doesn't want to know!"

Super dumb, Joe thought. "Forget it," he said. "I like your mother." He put his arm around Ellie. "Your mother's made you a good girl," he said matter-of-factly.

"How do you know if I'm good or not. Neither you nor my mother let me make any decisions."

34

"You don't have sense enough—and stop hugging me in public." He let his arm drop.

"Where're we going, Joe?"

"Walking."

"Where?"

"To the mountaintop."

"How come we can't go to Africa, like we usually do?"

Suddenly Joe didn't feel like playing. "I'm tired, Ellie," he said.

Ellie reached for his hand, squeezed his fingers gently, and said nothing. Neither of them spoke as they walked to Florida Avenue and turned the corner toward H Street.

In five minutes, they were mixed in with the sights and sounds of people, carry-out shops, pawnbrokers, record centers, food markets, more people, and the police of northeast Washington. One of the first areas to burn during the April rage of '68. The empty spaces, where buildings used to be, were now the homes of weeds peeking through dirt and ashes.

"Something's wrong, Joe. What is it?"

"I've been thinking."

"You're always thinking."

"I didn't want to, this time, but I couldn't stop. I left the job early today to do something. Only it didn't work out. I tried to make plans at school tonight, then tried *not* to make plans. Neither idea worked."

Ellie held on to his hand and looked at him.

Joe's white shirt, opened at the collar, made his skin

look an even deeper velvet black. His skin seemed to say this was the color to be, it was that dark and snooty. But tonight his mouth looked hard, the cleft in his chin rigid.

"Let's talk about us, Joe," Ellie said quietly. Then, with sudden brightness, she announced happily, "Summer's coming! When exactly do we leave for North Carolina?"

Joe didn't answer.

"I'm even packed already and we've got two more weeks to wait!" Ellie squeezed Joe's hand, pulled his whole arm up and placed it around her neck, and still held tight to his fingers. "We'd have all the summer to ourselves *if* you hadn't gone and got a campus job." She laughed, and pinched him. "So why'd you do it, Joe? Huh! Huh!"

Joe's heels against the pavement made a quiet sound.

"You saved enough money to pay your tuition two years! You don't need to work! But—what do you say? 'Ellie, I just can't lay up. I always had some kind of job.' But I say you don't have to work and you're just doing that to make me cut classes to spend time with you!" Ellie stopped walking long enough to kiss his cheek quickly. "I'll cut every single class," she murmured. But still Joe didn't respond.

"I'm not walking any further, Joe Brooks," Ellie finally announced, "until you tell me why you aren't talking and what's wrong and how many babies we're going to have when we're married!" She stopped walking.

Joe didn't.

Ellie caught up with him. "Joe, I'm not going to have a single son for you!"

"And you're a television kid," he said.

"A what?"

"A television kid going to college. Maybe you've got three relatives on the faculty. And one of them is president."

"I'm sorry, Joe," Ellie said quietly. "Let's not talk."

"You believe in dreams, Ellie. I don't."

"You believe in them too, Joe. You do. I know."

"But not the way you do. I don't trust make-believe, I can't deal that way. The only thing real right now is Thursday night. That's when I get that almighty high-school diploma you say will open up heaven. I don't know about heaven. I got Paul. And Paul says he got heaven. Says he can get it any time he wants."

"But Paul's all right now."

Joe didn't answer for a moment. "What's 'all right' mean, Ellie?"

"Joe, let's go to a record shop or something. Let's don't talk." Ellie's face brightened suddenly. "We can go to the park, to the wall, and you can tell me one of your wonderful stories. Then I'll be happy. Please, Joe, tell me a happy story. I don't want to talk about college or anything like that." The girl smiled and Joe felt like touching her, but he didn't. "Okay, Joe? Tell me a story?"

"No."

"Okay," she said. "I'm sorry. I keep saying the wrong things tonight. Let's just walk then. I'll be quiet. I promise."

Joe started laughing. "Wait! You want a story, I know a story. It's about a guy." It was an odd laugh and Ellie knew it and didn't laugh. "This must be a dumb cat, because he keeps on trying for something and he doesn't even know what he's trying for. His brothers know what they want, but not him. This cat's got a girl who makes him think he's a television teen. You know, knitted sweaters, shiny cars for Saturday dates, the whole family sitting down together for a 'birds and bees' conversation. You know, where the mother stays all dressed up and the father stands around with a pipe. I don't think the dude has a job! And the littlest kid in the house ends up telling everybody about life."

"Joe, don't—"

"No, listen, there's more. Let's go back to the brothers this cat has. One paints like God. But that's almost never now, unless he's on a super-high. He's too busy strung out on a line nobody can see but him. Then there's the other brother with everything going good for him, but he already knows he's out there alone. That ain't right, Ellie! Then there's a father who lets his woman run his life. And a mother who's convinced she's *got* to run it. And of course, there's the aunt." Joe smiled. "She can see the whole world in a little pouch she keeps with her. I looked in it one day, Ellie. All she had in there was a worn-thin wedding band that no longer fits over her finger. And a small faded piece of paper. Maybe an old note or something, I don't know. And a crumpled-up piece of string that was once a ribbon of a little girl who died while she was wearing it. I love Aunt Lou, because she's strong. They think she's crazy, but she's not. She really knows things. Sometimes at night she makes strange sounds. It's the sound of death, she says. And I believe it."

"Everything's going to be all right, Joe. That's what I believe!"

Joe looked at Ellie's soft face and for a moment he believed too. He wanted to hold on to that moment, so he stood there on the street and folded his arms about her. Her shoulders felt thin, like Paul's. But it was a better thin than his. Her hair smelled good. There were people watching and Joe saw them and didn't care and cared and was glad they saw.

He held her closer. "Once upon a time," he whispered, "there was a magic kingdom. In the middle of this kingdom lived a boy and girl who loved each other. She was pretty. And little. And silly. And she could make him believe anything. . . ."

An hour later, Joe and Ellie walked up the three flights of stairs to her apartment. She wanted to kiss him but he touched her hand instead and walked back downstairs into the warm spring night. Joe balled his hand into a fist, the hand that had touched her, and tried to hold on to what he felt. The way she felt.

He jammed this fist into his jacket pocket and carried the softness of Ellie home.

He opened the door to the sound of his mother's voice. Fussing.

4

"Brooks, I been working hard and doing all my life. I do the best I can. Even with you not able to work now, I'm still going on. And you know I don't complain about nothing that has to be. You want to think I do—but I don't." The long-limbed woman's hair, faded black and silvery, almost touched the top of the wide kitchen–dining-room doorway she was standing in. "When Llouvah came, did I complain? No! And tell me I don't do more for her than you ever did."

"Llouvah doing for Llouvah," came the sharp reply. Isaac Brooks reached from his chair at the dining-room table into the tiny alcove to pat his sister. But she drew up rigidly, smoothing the black material of her dress. "When Llouvah can't do, she be dead."

"Llouvah, I don't mean to upset you. Your brother's the one should be getting upset. But no indeed, don't nothing upset him! He's the one with a bad heart—but watch and see if it's not me they put in the grave!"

"Now, Mattie—"

"Mattie nothing. Don't 'Now, Mattie' me—'cause I begged you, Brooks. Absolutely begged you! Keep Paul in the house, I said, talk to him, I said. Paul hasn't been in this house seven months, that's what I said. I planned it, this dinner. We're all going to sit down together and eat and we're going to talk to him and show him everything's all right now. That's all I asked you—isn't that all I asked? But the minute I leave, what happens? The whole house falls apart."

Joe reached around David, who was rinsing dishes at the kitchen sink, washed his hands, and took a plate down from the cabinet.

"And in comes Mr. Cool, sashaying through the door, and don't say boo to nobody. Uh-uh, Joe, no—those two pieces of fish got lemon squeezed on it and you know you don't like lemon on your fish. That's for me and Paul. I'm not eating till he comes. Leave the wrapped up cornbread in the oven, and the two salads in the icebox with the foil on it. Paul's going to have a decent first meal at home and he's going to have somebody to sit down and talk to him too. That's me."

"Looks like a lot of people didn't eat besides you and Paul," Joe said.

"I didn't," David said. "I can wait."

"I can't," Joe said.

"No, naturally you can't—you're too cool for that!"

"I'm hungry, Momma. It's eleven o'clock." Joe felt a tightness in his stomach but it didn't have anything to do with hunger. He got another plate and filled it.

"What you doing?" his mother asked.

"Davey's finished the dishes. He's eating with me."

"David's waiting. He's eating with me and Paul!"

"He's eating with me too," Joe said.

David looked at Joe, shifted his eyeglasses, looked at his mother, and sat down at the kitchen table. Finally Mattie Brooks waved her arm at both her sons, went into the dining room, and sat down opposite her husband at the dining-room table. "Great brothers," she said. "That's what Paul got."

David was staring at the kitchen wall. He hadn't touched his food. "Eat your food, man," Joe said.

"Stuff your own face, but don't bug David. David was waiting with me."

"Mattie, leave the boys be. David can still eat a little something, if he wants to, when Paul comes. Though it seems to me everybody should have ate at the regular time, instead of this waiting."

"Brooks, don't you say nothing to me, you hear. David can do what he wants. I'm waiting! Paul's not going to eat alone this day."

"It's night, Mattie."

The tall woman reached across the table toward her husband. "What I care about night, Brooks?" she said, her voice shrill. "What I care about is my son!"

"Okay, Mattie, okay."

It was several moments before any of them realized she was crying, her long neck bowed, her head down. The quiet tears made the room seem smaller.

In the kitchen, David pushed his plate away.

"Eat," Joe said.

"I don't feel hungry."

"Nobody paid a bit of attention to him," Mattie was sobbing. "That's why he left. I know it. Everybody's talking and eating and acting like Paul still in the hospital. Like he don't exist! Joe walking in late as usual. And David, he had his head stuck down in a book and I ask him, 'Where's your brother, David?' and he says, 'He left after you went to work.' And I say, 'Where'd he go? What did he say he was going to do?' and I get the answer, 'I don't know, Momma.' Don't nobody ever know nothing about Paul. Only me."

Her husband put down the newspaper he was reading, got up, and turned on the television. He sat down with his back to his wife.

Mattie Brooks's head snapped back, and she jumped up from the table and thumped her husband on the back. Then she shoved him forward a little, but he didn't respond. "Television," she yelled. "That's your answer for everything, television and newspapers. And while you're reading, my son is in the street. Maybe if you *talked* to him he wouldn't have to go out to find somebody to talk to. One day Paul'll be rich. Then you'll talk to him. Oh, yeah!"

"Suppose he don't get rich, Momma," Joe called from the kitchen.

"Money don't mean nothing!" Mattie cried as she

44

stepped into the kitchen, her eyes narrowed and wet. "What I want is Paul happy! He's an artist—he's special, he's sensitive. He needs to know people care about him, love him, wish him well—that's what a family's for."

"We're all for Paul," Joe said.

"Paul's like my great-grandfather was," she said, ignoring Joe. "Your great-great-grandfather. Everybody in Georgia knew him. He'd sit and paint flowers and birds and people so real-looking folks would come from miles around to see. And he'd just give those beautiful pictures away. 'Matt-girl,' he'd say, 'you reckon you like this one?' and even though I was only a little girl, I'd talk to him about those pictures and he'd sit there, sometimes in a field, and just listen. He never talked to nobody like he talked to me."

"Joseph Matthew?"

"Yeah, Aunt Lou?"

"You finish eating?"

"Yeah, Aunt Lou," Joe said and got up and washed his plate in the cool soapy water. He turned away from the sink for a moment and winked across the dining room at his aunt in her little angular corner.

"When you seen Paul, how he look? When he out there waiting for you?"

Joe looked at his aunt. His mother also looked at her, then turned to Joe. "You see your brother, Joe?" she said. "You see Paul outside?"

"I saw him," Joe said.

45

"Oh, thank God," his mother said. Her voice, hoarse from crying, sounded brighter. "Why didn't you say so, Joe? You know how worried I am. Where'd he say he was going? What was he doing?"

"Eating Hersheys."

"What you mean, eating Hersheys?" she said quietly. She looked as if she wasn't breathing. "Did you stay with him, Joe? You try to help him?" She was almost mumbling.

David and his father were both staring at Joe. "No," Joe said.

Isaac Brooks turned back to the television.

"You're his brother," Mattie said, her voice rising. "How could you just walk away and leave him?"

"I was on my way to school."

"School!" she screamed. You *graduate* in a few days— you didn't need to go to no school tonight. You should have brought him home! He doesn't have to eat candy and drink sodas anymore. You knew the dinner I wanted to do here tonight and you see him and don't . . ." Mattie Brooks was unable to talk.

Joe turned back to the sink, rinsed and dried his plate, and was putting it back in the cabinet when his mother snatched him around. She was crying again. David got up and tried to put his arm around her, but she pushed him away.

"He doesn't have to be eating candy for the same reason he was eating it before, Momma," David said.

Joe walked out of the kitchen, and his mother followed. "You supposed to be so slick and so great, how come you didn't bring him home first? Then you could have gone about your business!"

"He said he was coming home then. I believed him. In a way, I believed him."

"What you mean, 'in a way'? What you trying to say?"

"Nothing, Momma."

Mattie Brooks almost struck Joe, but she stopped herself. Joe saw his mother's anger and understood it. David, standing in the doorway, looked at his brother. Joe ignored the look. He didn't need it. "Paul can have my life," he said finally.

"Oh, Lord Blessed Jesus!" his aunt screamed. She was standing up, her head thrown back, her eyes closed. She was holding the little leather pouch close to her throat, squeezing it with all her strength. Her large hands were rigid. "Lord Jesus, Joseph Matthew, child, don't be saying it!"

"I don't care, Aunt Lou."

A chilling scream came from the old woman but Joe hardly heard her.

"Stop that screaming, Llouvah!" Mattie yelled.

"What got to be, got to be, but that child ain't got to say it. He ain't got to say it." Aunt Lou's voice was low. She moved close to Joe and touched him, rubbed his back. "Joseph Matthew, child, get on 'way when you done graduating."

"Llouvah, don't you stand there scaring my son. What you mean, telling him to go? Nobody's going nowhere. Nothing in this house's going to hurt none of my children. I got a right to be mad. Joe could have made Paul come home. He could at least have tried!"

"Llouvah, Mattie—hush now, and Joe, you and David go on in the back and go to bed."

"Don't be hushing me. Llouvah don't need to tell my son to leave my house. You got something to say, say it to her!"

But Aunt Lou was walking down the hallway to the bathroom to begin her nightly washing of the thin rayon dress and the thick stockings.

Mattie was about to follow her when Paul walked in.

5

Mattie Brooks wasn't yelling now. Her voice was soft and soothing. "Paul, baby," she was saying. "Honey." She let her hand smooth his hair and slide down his neck, where she gave him a little pat. She touched the too-large sweater, rubbed his thin arm through the woolen cloth. "You all right?" she asked, standing close to Paul.

"Momma, you know where I was, Momma? Where I was, was over Bessie's. Me and Bessie. Bessie had a drink and I had a drink and then she had a drink and then I had a drink."

"That's all right, Paul, baby. That's fine. I'm glad you had somebody to talk to. You eat something? Bessie fix dinner for you?"

Paul was smiling past his mother, looking at Joe. "Little brother, sugar. You beat me home!"

"Yeah," Joe said, watching him.

"Eat a little something, Paul. A little fish—I saved it

for you, squeezed lemon on it for you. It's all wrapped up and warm and waiting for you. I saw that pretty boy you drew today. I'm taking him to work with me tomorrow so everybody can see him." She kissed Paul. "Those oils be out of layaway real soon. The salesman said those were the best oil paints money could buy, said you'd know the name."

But Paul wasn't listening. He had moved away from his mother and was clowning with David.

Then suddenly it was as if he didn't know who David was. His eyes, before he closed them, had a blank look.

Joe thought of Ellie. He remembered:

"But Paul's all right now."

"What's 'all right' mean, Ellie?"

Mattie Brooks no longer looked so loving. She looked scared. Like something was terribly out of control. "Paul, baby, honey."

"Momma, my beautiful," Paul said, putting his arms about his mother in a loose hug. He laid his head on her shoulder and kept it there until Mattie took his face in her hands.

Suddenly Paul brightened. He looked at David as if David had not been standing there all along. "Throw me one, Dave!" he shouted. It wasn't a loud shout. Paul's throat had lost the ability to make extreme sounds. "Throw me one, man, since you supposed to have the best arm in D.C. Throw me one, sugar!" Paul started faking basketball shots.

50

David returned the fake play but he kept an eye on his mother.

She was watching Paul.

Paul dove for David's legs, as though to wrestle. "Deal with this, man," he said, laughing, "deal with this."

David tried to untangle Paul from his legs without being too rough. It was like playing with a fragile, delicate thing, Joe thought.

Mattie was beginning to look disgusted. "I'm trying to get him to eat," she said. "Stop playing." She glared at David.

"Cut it out, Paul," David pleaded gently. "Let's go. Come on, man, get up. Get up and eat your food. Come on, I don't want to hurt you."

"Hurt me! Sugar, you can't even talk!" Paul held fast to David's legs.

They fell against the dining-room table.

"David! Go to bed or something. Go on back in your room!" Mattie ordered.

Paul let go. He gave David's retreating figure an elaborate salute, then sat down at the dining-room table and looked at his father. "Where's Aunt Lou?" he asked of no one in particular.

"In the bathroom," his mother answered.

"Hey, Pop!" Paul said suddenly. "How you doing?"

The father said nothing. And Joe, who had begun ironing a pair of khaki's just before the scuffle, looked up just in time to see Paul's eyes close. "Hey, little brother,"

Paul said with his eyes shut, "we going to write some books, sugar."

Mattie set a beautifully arranged plate of fish, baked potato, and collard greens topped with bacon strips in front of Paul. She placed a salad with blue-cheese dressing on one side of the plate and a dish with buttered cornbread on the other. "Eat, baby," she said and put her own plate beside his. "Eat. And that whisky you drank won't make you so sleepy. There's nothing wrong with a little drinking with your friends to celebrate your being home. I can understand that."

Paul opened his eyes. "My beautiful mother," he said, "my ebony queen. I ate already, biggest steak sandwich you ever did see. Had some fries and a milk shake—no, check that. I had me three milk shakes. Vanilla and chocolate and strawberry."

Isaac Brooks turned away from the television and looked at Paul.

"The chocolate one was the best." Paul grinned.

"Came through a needle too, didn't it, Paul?" his father said.

"If Paul said he ate, he ate!" Mattie screamed.

The man leaned forward and turned the television off. For a moment, Joe thought his father would say something. But he didn't. He reached for his newspaper and began to read.

David came back into the dining room. "The counselor set up another appointment, Momma. It's tomorrow. He really has to talk to you."

"David, look, don't bother me—right now, I just can't think. I said I was coming up, didn't I?"

"But, Momma, you said that before. School's almost over and somebody has to come."

Isaac Brooks looked up. "What is it, David?" he asked. "What are you talking about?"

"Nothing, Pop," David said.

"I'm taking care of it, Brooks. You just keep right on sitting and reading and doing nothing!"

David hesitated. "It's very important to me," he said.

"Everything's important this week! Paul's home, Joe's graduating, and the school wants to see me about you. If you smart enough for this thing, why is it they got to talk to me about it?" She sighed deeply, disgusted. "Okay! Okay. I'll go tomorrow."

"What time?"

"Damn!"

"It's important, Momma."

"David! Go on back in your room. It's time for you and everybody else to be in bed. And look at those pajamas—I just bought them a few weeks ago and you've outgrown them already. Go to bed."

David walked out after a moment and Joe wondered what the school thing was all about. He folded up the ironing board, put it away, and was walking back to the bedroom when his mother called his name. "Make Paul eat, Joe. He listens to you. Make him eat."

Paul was still sitting at the table, eyes closed, head bowed over the full plate of food.

Joe touched his brother.

"Hey, where's Dave?" Paul said, pushing away from the table. "Dave think he can wrestle somebody!"

Mattie started toward her son, but Paul was on his way to the back bedroom.

Joe watched his mother take the plates off the table, wrap everything up again, and put it in the refrigerator.

He was not surprised when she came out of the kitchen with another plate. Empty, and shining clean. Along with a knife, spoon, fork, and paper napkin. She set a single place. It was for Paul. "We've got to stick by him and encourage him and let him know how much we love him. I don't care about his drinking. I can take that. I can take anything but him using that heroin stuff again. God knows I'd like to kill the person who invented it! But I watched him tonight and I know whisky'll make you act just like he's acting. I know it. I've seen it. Your father didn't have no business talking about needles. I think maybe he said that just to scare Paul a little."

She went into the kitchen.

Joe felt the crawling feeling moving about in his insides again. Weaving through his brain. He sat down in the chair nearest the wide doorway and watched his mother make two massive meat sandwiches and wrap them in foil.

"Get the Magic Marker, Joe."

Joe opened the buffet drawer, got the marker, and gave it to her.

54

She carefully printed the letters P A U L on each sandwich. Then she stuck them in her "icebox." Joe couldn't ever remember his mother saying "refrigerator." She'd say "You defrost the icebox," or "Take all that mess off the top of my icebox."

"Now Paul'll have something if he gets hungry during the night," she announced, somewhat to herself.

Then she wrote a note and laid it on top of the dinner plate. The note said:

DEAR PAUL, PLEASE EAT THE SANDWICHES I MADE FOR YOU IN THE ICEBOX. LOVE, MOMMA

Then, as an afterthought, she had written:

STAY HOME FOR ME TOMORROW AND DRAW ME A PRETTY PICTURE. I LOVE YOU ALWAYS.

Right then, at that moment, Joe wanted to hold his mother in his arms. To tell her not to worry about Paul, maybe to worry more about herself. But she would not have allowed it and he knew it.

"The fact is," Joe said, "that whether or not Paul wants to eat has nothing to do with it. Paul's stomach won't take those sandwiches, Momma. Not tonight."

"Don't be telling me now about Paul's stomach! A few minutes ago, when I asked you to help me make him eat, you stood there looking and didn't do nothing. So you can forget it now. He's got to eat, he's got to! Most of Paul's treatment at the hospital was getting good food.

Eating well. Tomorrow morning I'll get up and make him a real good breakfast before I go to work. But tonight, if he needs it, he's got these sandwiches."

Mattie looked at her husband. "I'm going to bed," she said. She turned out every light except the one he needed to read by, and walked toward the hallway to the bedrooms. "Go to bed, Joe. And don't be talking to Paul all night. He needs his rest."

Joe went into the kitchen, reached into the cabinet, and got a small bottle of pills. He put it on the table near his father.

"I'll take it in a minute. You go to bed, son."

But Joe got some orange juice from the refrigerator, poured some in a tall glass, and set it down by the pills.

"Joseph?"

"Yeah, Pop?"

"Keep an eye on your clothes and stuff, just in case Paul wasn't drinking. I got a funny feeling."

Later, Joe lay in bed and thought, I got a funny feeling too, Pop.

He listened to his brothers breathe.

Once, he got up and pushed David's feet back under the blanket. David's feet were always sticking out from under covers.

He watched tree shadows flicker across his books on the dresser. He'd have to turn them in tomorrow.

David's books were piled on the dresser too, his eyeglasses on top.

Paul had tried to pawn them once.

No one was certain whether Paul hadn't found a willing pawnbroker, whether the glasses were not pawnable, or whether Paul had just thought better of it. He had simply come into the house with them, said he'd tried to pawn them and couldn't.

Joe remembered buying the glasses. He thought of what had happened when David had come home from school with the small yellow slip requesting glasses for him.

"Two seconds looking at a chart isn't enough time for nobody to be sure a person needs glasses! Those people checking children's eyes in school don't have no medical training."

"Mattie, if he got a note like that, he needs glasses. Go to the bank for the money, get him checked out again at a good eye doctor, and get what he needs."

"Brooks, the first thing you think about is bank money. I don't need to go there to get money to take him to no doctor and get nobody's eyeglasses—I work every day. That's where I get money for eyeglasses!"

"I don't need glasses, Momma. I can see okay."

"Don't tell me. You should have told them."

"I'll take him, Mattie."

"Brooks, don't you say nothing. How you going to sit all day at Children's Hospital waiting to see an eye doctor? You know you not well enough. Soon's I get a minute, I'll take him."

Joe smiled when he thought of David at the store.

"How they feel, man? You like the way they look?"

"Thanks, Joey."

"That ain't what I asked you, man. How they feel and can you see all right?"

"I can see."

"Better than before?"

"Better than before."

"Good. Now, Mr. Optician, how much?"

"Seventy-two dollars. You got my best frames and he needed a pretty hefty prescription."

"Here's your seventy-two and me and my brother want a case."

"They're stamping his initials on it. It'll only take a minute. Listen, young man. David. At fourteen—how tall are you?"

"Six-two."

"Play basketball?"

"I play a little."

"What he means is he plays a lot and plays it good. Sure as that dashiki you wearing, he plays it good!"

"Good luck."

"He got it, man."

Joe remembered what his mother had said later.

"Didn't nobody tell Joe to go buy those glasses, but I'm glad he did. It's his brother! Joe's working, and buying glasses is better than buying a lot of mess and wasting money."

"Davey looking good now, ain't he, Aunt Lou!"

"You a man, Joseph Matthew."

"Cool, Aunt Lou."

"How much, Joseph?"

"Don't remember, Pop."

Joe looked over at Paul's thin body beneath the blue chenille bedspread. His long slim fingers were spread out as if he were touching something wide. Except for the fact that he was a man, he had the same face as his mother.

Suddenly Paul sat up and swung his needle-marked legs over the side of the bed. "Little brother," he said, "you and Dave do it good, 'cause I won't make it."

"You're going to make it, Paul. We'll all make it."

"Not me, sugar."

"Why?"

"I just don't care."

"Why?"

Paul lay back down on the bed. He lay still for so long that Joe finally looked away.

"You ever have a woman?" Joe heard Paul say softly. "A real woman. A woman so fine, man, you've never seen nothing like what she's got and she gives you so much good feeling that you want to bust yourself wide open? That's what it is, little brother, that's what it is."

No, Paul, Joe thought. That ain't it. A woman like that would make you look good. You look bad.

"I see only good things when I close my eyes. It's beautiful, sugar.

"I can see Momma pushing me in a baby carriage and

59

buying me ice cream and you too, man. When I taught you the Pledge of Allegiance you wasn't but two-and-a-half years old and you said it right and I was proud. See, when I close my eyes I can see you saying that Pledge of Allegiance much as I want. And I can see Dave learning to walk. Remember how we use to jive around with him trying to make him walk? You remember, little brother?"

"I remember, Paul."

"Remember that day he took off? You remember?"

"Yeah, I remember."

"It was beautiful, man, seeing him fall and keep getting up. It was great. And Dave still getting it on, man. He ain't never looked back. He's steady-dealing good."

Paul was quiet for a moment.

"But it's pain too," he finally said. "What hurts is when you coming back and realize where you been."

Paul's voice was fading.

"Paul!"

"Yeah, little brother! What you yelling for?" His voice was quick and alert.

"How come you had to do it, get on?"

Paul laughed. "Like you say, little brother—'Once upon a time.' Well, once upon a time I had a heavy need."

"Why?"

Paul didn't answer.

"Everybody black got a heavy need, man. But pumping that stuff ain't the answer." Joe waited but still Paul said nothing.

"How come you come out, long as you been away, and go right back on it? 'Cause you on it, Paul!"

"No, I'm not. Not on nothing hard. I had some drinks and a few reefers."

"Reefers don't make you act like you acting."

"You wrong."

"What about the OD, man—didn't it scare you? You almost died."

"It scared me, but when you dying, you don't think about it. Being scared I mean." Paul sat and thought for a while. "Everybody got to die," he said finally.

Joe wanted to say something but he didn't know what. He would have beaten Paul senseless if it would have helped. Maybe the feeling he had was wrong, maybe the coldness moving through his stomach now while he watched Paul meant nothing. Maybe his mother was right. Maybe all they had to do was love him more. But Paul already knew that anybody in the house would have died for him if it was necessary.

"Those books we're doing will be something else, little brother. The kind we doing is kids' books, the best stories and faces of black kids anybody ever saw. Know what, little brother? You ever see the faces of children in flowers, man? I mean look right on down in and see the faces? Beautiful."

Paul sat halfway off the bed, staring, saying nothing. After a while, Joe fell asleep, watching him.

When Joe woke up, Paul was drawing the face of a woman.

Her hair was natural and lush and voluptuous. Piercing black diamond eyes, wisdom-fired, were set deep in black onyx skin. She was a nation place, a man and child place.

At first Joe didn't see the smile. Then he did, and marveled at his brother's skill.

He pretended to sleep, so that the slim fingers moving so deftly wouldn't stop.

Paul wasn't fooled. "Do me a thing?" he said.

"What's that, Paul?"

Paul settled back. "Buy her a deep-brown wooden frame. Not too thick, else it'll take away from her—I want it plain."

"Okay."

"Little brother?"

"Yeah."

"She ain't to match no furniture. Africa womb—that's what she is. Great Momma of Black America."

"I can dig it," Joe said quietly.

When he woke up again it was daylight and Paul was gone. Joe's pillow seemed suddenly hard as he stared at Africa womb, Momma of Black America.

Joe got up and sat on David's bed. "Davey," he said softly. "Hey, Davey!"

David jumped, and when he saw Joe's face he seemed startled. "What's wrong?"

"This counselor business you were asking Momma about last night—what's it all about?"

"Oh, yeah," David said, sitting up in bed. "It's a chance for me to get on a special program. But it doesn't start until September, when I'm a senior."

"That all you got to say about it?"

"I'll get a chance to go away on trips, some by airplane, to classes in other cities. You work on city planning projects, stuff like that. The best part is you get to visit a lot of colleges and universities and stay there for a few days and look around and talk to people." David grinned. "I was lucky they thought about me. They only picked nine kids from D.C."

Joe kept his eyes on David's face. "What you mean about it almost being too late?"

"I told Momma about it a long time ago. I didn't want to bother Pop. You know how he gets when he goes out— he can hardly breathe. So, I was waiting for Momma to take a day off, but she didn't have time. And now, it's the last week."

"We go today," Joe said.

"You can't do it, Joey. The papers have to be notarized, because the school's going to pay my expenses. I'm eligible for it because Pop's disabled and all, but they have to have proof of family income first."

"How come you didn't tell me about it?"

David smiled a wide smile. "I wanted to surprise you," he said.

"We go today," Joe said again and walked out of the bedroom.

63

Joe thought about it while he showered, and decided that there wasn't anything very surprising about David's being picked for a special senior year. It just seemed to fit. Nor was he surprised at his mother's words, twenty minutes later.

"Don't come out here telling me what to do, Joe. I said I'd see about it, but not today!"

"Okay," Joe said. "Okay."

But when his mother walked to the bus stop, on the way to work, Joe was walking beside her. "I called your job," he said. "They're not expecting you till this afternoon."

Mattie Brooks stopped walking. Her mouth opened angrily.

"Don't get mad," Joe said. "It's Paul."

Immediately her face softened. "Paul? What's wrong? Where's Paul? Where is he!"

"I don't know. When I came outside, on my way to work, I saw Bunky and he said Paul had been sitting on the basement steps crying. So I called my job, called yours, and waited for you to come downstairs." Joe lied carefully.

"Call Bessie! You know Bessie's number, call it."

"I did already. He's not there."

"I'm scared, Joe. I'm real scared for Paul—why would he want to sit down on the steps and cry? He knew I was upstairs." Joe saw his mother tremble a little.

"We'll find him."

64

"Where? Where we going?"

"Walking, Momma. And riding busses."

Mattie did very little talking on the busses, but talked constantly as they walked. Finally her voice broke, and she started to cry. "Who knows what he went through at that hospital? God only knows what that treatment was about and what it did to him. I never trusted it. I knew I was right when I saw him still skinny and not eating nothing."

His mother's tears bothered Joe a little, but he kept walking. It had been necessary to tell her the lie about Paul. Paul wouldn't mind, he was sure of that. And his mother had plenty of leave. She never took off from work.

The lie had been important, to help David.

"Paul used to hang around Davey's school a lot. Let's try it, then we'll go over Bessie's and wait awhile."

The dark school corridor was quiet. Joe remembered the office well. He had quit school a million years ago, leaning over this same brown-metal counter. "Maybe we can take care that business Davey told you about last night while we here. He said his stuff's the only one not done yet." Joe turned to the office clerk seated on the other side of the counter. "The eleventh-grade counselor's office," Joe asked, "is it still down the hall on the other side of the boys' bathroom?"

"Joe, no! We got to find Paul. I don't have time to talk to nobody."

"Yes," the clerk said. "You have an appointment?"

"No," Mattie said to her, "we don't have an appointment and we didn't come to see him today. I want to see my son, David Brooks. Can you get him to the office, please?"

"Oh!" the clerk said, smiling. "You're David Brooks's mother." After checking a card file, she walked over to the public address microphone. Her voice sounded muffled through the old equipment. She clicked it off and walked back smiling. "I know you're proud of him!"

"Is he coming straight down?"

"Yes. I called his class. He'll be here in a minute. You know, I just typed up the program for the eleventh-grade final assembly and I think he took most all the awards. But don't tell him!"

"I can't tell none of them nothing," Mattie said. "This one here's trying to get me to do one thing when I'm here for something else."

Joe steered his mother out of the office. "We'll wait in the hall," he said to the clerk.

"We ought to take David with us to find Paul. That'll be three looking."

"No, Momma," Joe said. "We're not looking for Paul. That was a lie I made up to get you here."

"You what!"

"I didn't even see Bunky."

"You mean you wasted my time, had me walking all over for nothing? Called my job for nothing!" Her voice was rising with every word.

"Don't get excited, Momma. Do this for Davey, please. It'll only take a few minutes. You're already here."

"I told David what I'd do!" she said, walking toward the exit. Joe caught up with her.

"Go down to the counselor's office, Momma. All you got to do is talk to the cat five minutes!"

But his mother, without looking back or answering, walked through the wide door to the street.

David appeared as the door swung closed.

"Hey, Joey."

Joe smiled to keep his brother from knowing something was wrong. "Hey, baby," he said. "It's counselor's office time! We can get the stuff you worrying about and take it home to get it signed. Then when Momma comes she can just do the talking."

"It has to be notarized, Joey."

"I can get anything you want notarized," Joe said. "So let's go."

"What you doing with books?"

"It's turning-in time tonight," Joe whispered, and playfully slapped his brother's back. "Ain't that good?"

An hour later, Joe placed David's completely notarized papers back into the manila school envelope and tucked it into his Black History textbook. The forms had neither the information filled in nor the necessary signatures.

That night, the papers, filled in and signed and folded neatly in the envelope, were lying on the dining-room table when Joe's mother woke him up.

"Joe," she begged, "help me. Paul is sick. He looks

bad. I got to get him to the hospital and you're the only one I can depend on. Your father won't go, you know that, and David can't do anything. Please help me," she cried. "Please!"

Joe got out of bed and reached for his clothes.

"Hurry!"

"Where is he?"

"In the hallway. Leaning way down."

6

"I don't think we can help him here," the tired-looking nurse at the desk said. "You'll have to take him to the city hospital. We don't take—"

"He's just sick," announced Mattie Brooks. "Just sick and I want the doctor to see him. You can't turn us away. It's the law and I know it. I used to work in a hospital too. Long time ago, maybe—but things haven't changed that much. You just make up a chart, and we'll wait till the doctor calls us."

The nurse glared at Joe's mother. But the uniform, white against black skin, was no threat to Mattie Brooks. She feared no one where Paul was concerned.

Finally Joe heard the nurse say, "What is his name, please?" and his mother answer, "Thank you very much, miss. His name is Paul. Paul Edwards Brooks."

Writing the history took a while, because nurse and mother couldn't agree. In the end, "artist" was listed as occupation, though the nurse added "unemployed," and the reason for emergency was listed as "stomach trouble." But Joe saw the nurse add something else. In bold letters, she printed, PATIENT LETHARGIC, EYES CLOSED. BENDING. STOOD STRAIGHT ONCE BUT NOT ALERT. SUSPECTED DRUG ADDICTION, POSSIBLY HEROIN.

His mother hadn't noticed.

They waited for the doctor a long time. Paul stood against the wall in a deep nod. Several people watched, obviously fascinated. Joe figured it must be the first time they'd seen a junkie. After a while, he stopped caring whether they looked or not.

It was a busy, moving, come-one, come-all place. Two women expecting babies arrived. One was into a deep drug nod and Paul was temporarily relieved of all stares. She was put in a mobile bed and wheeled away.

The other woman was having fun. Her husband shook his head at her and smiled while she talked. "Every time I turn around, I'm having another baby! I'm the only woman left still having 'em. I got me more babies than anybody here, I bet." The woman she singled out to speak to was obviously embarrassed, but there was no way to ignore the booming voice. "How many kids you got, honey?"

"None."

"None! Here, take my husband. He's good—brings his money home and loves babies!"

The woman looked even more embarrassed.

"He does all the naming. My children got the prettiest names in D.C. The last even got an African name—and he's got a pretty one this time, if it's a girl." She turned to him again. "Tell them the name, honey. You know you want to tell them."

He kissed her. "Ebony," he said, smiling.

"Ain't that something—I tell you he sure can pick them all right!"

When she was safely in a wheel chair, her husband pushed her carefully down the hall. "You don't have to tell him where to push me, nurse," Joe heard the woman say. "He's pushed me down this hall nine times already!"

Joe liked them. It was better to remember their joy than to look around at eyes. The eyes were full of stories and Joe could read some of them. He was listening to a young revolutionary protesting "capitalistic hospitals" when he heard his brother's name called.

"Oh, thank God," Mattie said, greatly relieved. "The doctor in that room came out once—he's black, and God knows I'm glad. A black doctor'll be able to understand and help Paul better. Get Paul, Joe, and walk him straight as you can. Don't say nothing—let me do all the talking."

But Joe saw that his mother's talking wasn't doing any good.

"We can't keep him here," the doctor said.

"You've *got* to help him, doctor. He can't help himself."

"What do you want me to do?"

"Why you asking me? I'm not the doctor. He's sick—
he needs to be in a hospital where they can force him to
eat."

"I'm sorry," the doctor said, running his fingers
through the silvery sides of his Afro. "If we put every
addict on the street in a hospital, there would be no
room for anybody else, and that wouldn't be the answer
to the problem."

"Let's go home, Momma," Joe said.

"You shut up," his mother said as Paul straightened
up a little, then bent forward again. "Just shut up!"

But the doctor turned to Joe. "He ever been detoxified,
or on a rehabilitation program? What about methadone?"

"He just came out the hospital," Joe said quietly.
"Sunday."

"This Sunday? Four days ago?"

"Yes, sir."

"He's been away, yes!" Mattie said. "But they didn't
do nothing for him. He needs to be in a regular hospital
like this. Please, can't you keep him here, doctor, and
help him? It's not a hard thing to do to help him. I'm
begging you."

"I'm sorry. I can't make a space for him. Take him
home tonight and let him sleep. Then I think you should
contact the people who just recently helped him. Maybe
they have an answer."

"No! What they got is nothing! I'll help him myself—
I'll help him if I have to spend the night going to every

hospital in D.C.!" Mattie was crying now. "He's an artist, doctor. Joe! Tell the doctor that."

Joe said nothing.

"No. You have to stand there and look simple," she cried roughly. Then she turned to the doctor and lowered her voice. "You should see the pictures he draws. The people look so real. Just like they can talk. Like they can walk right off the paper. My great-grandfather was like that and I just wish he could have lived to see Paul."

Her tears slowed but her voice was shaking. "Paul's a gift to this family and we have to do something to help him. I know if he ate and gave that stuff something to soak into, he'd be better. But he don't. He don't eat nothing."

"He's got to help himself," the doctor said. "He has to want to stop. Any idea why he started taking drugs?"

"Told me he needed it," Joe said.

"Don't tell that lie, Joe! Paul didn't need no drugs. He didn't need nothing like that. Anything he ever needed I tried to give him. He knew that. I wanted him to be a great artist, just like he wanted."

"And what do you want?" the doctor asked Joe.

For a moment, Joe couldn't answer. His voice, like his body, seemed apart from him. Apart and disconnected like fragments of a torn photograph. A picture of a birthday party, his birthday party. Of his father, big and strong, teasing his mother. Of Paul laughing a real laugh. And Davey watching ice cream melt in his hand.

73

His mother's face and the soundlessness of Paul, mixed with the sweat running down his stomach and back, and Joe remembered where he was. "To live," he said.

"Joe don't need nobody. He never did. David neither. It's Paul I got to help. Or die!" Mattie Brooks, her eyes wet and swollen, put her arm firmly around Paul's thin waist and moved toward the door.

Joe paid for the cabs to two other hospitals and finally for the one going home. But the crawling feeling he had felt was gone now. For him, the trouble curtain had lifted and he could see. The clear answer had come and he was glad. He was calm.

Things were clearer for Paul too. He was alert and angry. He refused to go in the house with his mother and left. Almost dragging his mother down the street with him.

Joe caught up and touched his brother's arm. "I think you're great, Paul, and you know I always did," he said. "But I can't worry about you anymore. It's over between you and me." Joe could hear his mother screaming, could feel her pushing him, hitting him.

"Little brother, man." Paul's voice was very weak. "Give me a break, sugar."

Joe had wanted to, but it was too late now. "You're wasted," he said. "You went away seven months and came right back and jumped on that needle again. And I wanted to believe you, wanted to believe your whisky and grass lie. But it wasn't no whisky, wasn't no reefers. It was the needle, man. Pure needle!"

Joe felt his mother's arms around his waist pulling him backward, away from Paul. Easily, and as gently as he could, Joe unhooked her arms. "I believed in you for three whole days. Now it's over." Joe reached out and folded his arms tight around his brother, tears in his eyes. "I'm leaving, Paul. I got to go—so Davey can make it. I can't give him much, but what I got to give is enough to help him for a while."

"Dave ain't like us, little brother. He's solid, man. He's gonna be okay."

"That's right," Joe said. "But I want you to know, you don't count no more. You understand? You understand that?"

"Solid. I understand."

Following Joe up the stairs, Mattie was hysterical. "I could kill you, Joe! You talked to him like a dog!"

"He understands."

"I don't! I don't understand!" she screamed.

Joe stopped on the steps and looked at his mother. "What do you think about me, Momma?" he asked.

"Think! I don't think nothing!"

"And Davey? What you think about Davey?"

"David's no trouble. You don't hear me complain about David. But soon's he grows up, he'll be messing around just like you!"

Joe's calm voice was even calmer when he spoke. "Momma, I'd like you to know that Davey is very smart. He's got a mind-blowing outasight brain. All his teachers have told you that, they've been telling you that since he was in kindergarten. Davey is as great as Paul. Davey is a 'gift,' as you say. Besides being smart, he's a natural athlete. And just a good, clean chump—and I love him. Like I love Paul. But Paul's not coming through because for some reason he's given up. So, Davey's the one. Davey is it!"

"Sure he's smart. You were smart too. But that didn't mean nothing! You dropped out of school anyway."

"But does it matter, to you, that I got back in? And that I held a full-time job the whole time and did the best I could for two long years? Does it matter, to you, that I'm graduating tomorrow night?"

"Big deal!" she said, pushing past him on the steps. "Night school!"

"And that's a disappointment to you isn't it, Momma?"

Mattie Brooks stopped and looked back. "It's not my life, it's yours."

"I'm joining the Navy today, Momma. And I'm going to leave as soon as I can."

"Good," she said. "Good luck to you!"

But later that morning, Mattie Brooks spoke gently to her son—touched his neck, hugged him. "Don't leave me, Joe," she pleaded. "I won't know what to do without you here. You don't need to join no Navy. I'm sorry for what I said. I'm so sorry, Joe." She kissed him.

Joe couldn't remember the last time she had done that.

"You can't leave," she whispered. "Paul needs you. You and I can pull him through this thing. I know it!"

She was rubbing Joe's hand. "If he gets another overdose, he might die!"

Before daybreak, Joe, watching David's long form in bed, sat down in the half-dark and wrote him a letter:

Dear Davey,

You're going to need a lot of things after I leave. Some of them, money can buy.

So, I'm giving you that.

A year from now, when you start college, this little piece of money will help you begin it—without begging anybody.

I know you'll use it right, but if you don't, it won't matter—it's yours to do what you want with, no strings attached. Except two.

First, when you got this cash in your pocket, don't wear no wrinkled shirts. And second, keep your eye on whatever it is you're working so hard for. Don't give up on it. It must be pretty important, if I know you.

In a way, I wish you'd tell me. But maybe it's best to keep people out your business. I can dig that. So, even though you never said what it was, promise me you'll do it.

The college thing just isn't for me right now, but maybe it will be, later in my life. I know it would never mean to me anyway what it would mean to you. You're a college kind of dude, Davey, and I'm not knocking it. You take to books like you a book yourself. But I dig people. That's my thing. I know you dig people too, but you cooler with it than me.

So the money's for you, because Momma's not going to get up off anything extra, except maybe for Paul. So you got to think of yourself.

Listen to Paul. But don't believe in him too much—he'll let you down. And don't trust him—it'll only get you off your road. He's not the brother we grew up with. Sometimes you'll look at Paul and want to cry, but that won't help him and it won't help you. I know, because I tried it. But I can't cry for him anymore. If anything I'd cry for you.

Most of all, don't let Momma throw you. She means you no harm, she loves you. But don't wait to hear her say it. She won't. And then again, she does, in her way. I think you know, by now, to see it when it comes. Her love, I mean.

She just happens to have a favorite, it's as simple as that. Maybe when you're a father, you'll have a favorite too. But I doubt it. You'll know how hard it is on the rest.

Keep an eye on Pop. And respect him, because he's the one you'll have when I leave. Don't think because he takes a lot, he's not a man, because he is. He'll understand your problems. Learn to talk to him.

And every time you can, hug Aunt Lou. Don't think she's crazy, 'cause she's not. What she is, is a grand lady. Believe what she says.

Just be a man, Davey. That's all I want. Do what you got to do and don't let no kind of nothing turn you around, and I'll be so proud. Just do that for me.

I wish I could stay around and watch you grow but I can't. I've got some growing to do myself. Just understand that I had to get away. I had to leave for you, so you can get it on. This was the only way I knew.

And when you're down and feeling bad and think you need somebody, think of me and know how much I love you and how much I want you to go right on.

Your brother,
Joe

Joe put the letter in his drawer. He'd get the money out of the bank today.

7

The U.S. Navy Recruiting Station, downtown Washington, was not fancy.

Joe had expected flags flying, scale models of great battleships, portraits of famous officers, and a band playing.

But what he saw were paper forms neatly stacked in massive piles, severely sharpened navy-blue pencils, and U.S. Navy gold-stamped ball-point pens.

Joe thought the whole place looked overprepared.

A black officer welcomed him. "When will you be eighteen?" he asked, shortly after Joe sat down.

"August fourteenth."

"You need the permission of both—"

"They'll sign."

Joe realized he had spoken too quickly. He saw Officer James C. Thomas, SMC, USN, looking at him carefully.

"How about enjoying the summer with your girl and coming back here the day after August fourteen?"

"Summer's not important," Joe said. "I want to get away."

"Summer was pretty important when I was your age."

Joe ignored the comment. "How soon can I leave if I bring back the papers today?"

"You have to do a few things first. And you can't get started on them until Friday."

"This Friday?"

"Yes, this Friday."

"Good," Joe said.

Officer Thomas settled back in his chair. "We send recruits to Baltimore three times a week. Mondays, Wednesdays, and Fridays."

"Friday's O.K. with me. Where do I go in Baltimore?"

"You don't go to Baltimore. You come here first and get your papers. Then a special bus will take you and the rest of the recruits to Baltimore and bring you back here. Lunch will be provided."

"How long after that can I leave?" Joe laughed then. "You know, like I'd like to see the world."

"Okay, good! The first part of your world will be, as I said, in Baltimore, where you'll get a physical examination and a mental examination—"

"I'll pass. Then what happens?"

"A lot of tests—reading, arithmetic, and some mechanical reasoning. You'll be told to take apart something simple and you'll be responsible for putting it back together correctly. They watch the way you follow directions and also a record will be made of much of what you say and do. Be aware of this."

A down black dude, Joe thought. I like him.

"Depending on your scores, there will or will *not* be other forms to complete."

"Then what? I mean if I do all right in Baltimore?"

"You can leave in two weeks."

"Two weeks!"

"Or we can grant you a deferment for up to a hundred and twenty days."

"Forget the deferment. Even two weeks is too long."

"I wish I could be more useful. I'm sorry."

"You doing all right."

After that, it was a matter of filling out forms. Twice the officer asked if Joe needed help. Joe didn't, and twenty minutes later it was over.

"Joseph Matthew Brooks," Officer Thomas announced, extending his hand, "the United States Navy expects you here on Friday morning."

Joe shook the officer's hand.

"You'll be here?"

"I'll be here," Joe answered. But he turned back when he got to the door. "How goes the Navy on black?"

"Like the rest of America. Can you deal with that?"

"Yeah," Joe said, "I can deal."

"Good," the officer said. "Next stop, Baltimore."

No, Joe thought as he walked through the downtown crowd, next stop is quit my job and then buy a few things and go to the bank.

Then Joe changed his mind. First stop was the bank.

8

"How do you want this?" the teller asked. "Cash or cashier's check?"

"Cash," Joe said.

Quitting his job was next.

Joe had planned to spend only a few minutes there, but it took him longer than that. His supervisor was an old Navy man.

"I remember the ride from Union Station to the United States Naval Training Center in Great Lakes, Illinois," he told Joe. "I was in Company Sixty-seven there. We made the Hall of Fame and got featured in the yearbook, so when you get there and look through that little blue book—you'll see a picture of me carrying the flag."

"I go to Baltimore first."

"Baltimore! No, sir, not in my day. Then it was from here straight to Illinois. I was sure some scared puppy on that train and I didn't even have a winter coat. I was wearing one of my father's old jackets. I was puny then, didn't have this stomach! And black folks weren't wearing a bush then, so I had me a skinny. You try to look at that picture, 'cause I know you'll have to go to Great Lakes."

After a while, Joe got away and went to personnel. When it was over, he left. It was time to shop and Joe took a cab to his favorite place. An expensive, black-owned, men's boutique.

The quiet, soothing voice of Jerry Butler sliding from hidden speakers, and the soft, deep plush carpeting relaxed Joe.

He bought a pale-beige knit suit, a white shirt, a brown and white striped tie, chocolate-colored ribbed socks that didn't need garters, and a pair of Edwin Clapp midnight-brown dress boots.

At the jewelers, he bought something for Ellie. It took him longer than he'd thought it would to find a dress he liked for his mother, and he got to Ellie's school just in time.

She came out looking silly. "Hey! Ooooh, packages! Can I peek?"

"*May* I peek."

" 'May' I peek in the packages?"

"No."

"I know everything in it's brown anyway!"

"Wrong. I'm trying navy blue."

"You lying, Joe!"

Joe kept a serious face.

"Tell you what," she said. "If the clothes you bought, the ones in the bag, are blue—you aren't coming to your graduation tomorrow night. If they're brown, you are."

"You think you know me, don't you, Ellie?"

"I know the stuff you just bought is brown."

Joe looked at her and laughed. "You win," he said.

"How come you buy so much brown?"

"Looks good with black."

"You're conceited!"

"Right."

"Since I guessed, let me peek!"

"No."

"You're mean, Joe," Ellie said, trying to look sad.

"You're right," he said.

"Tell me how good you're going to look while I'm sitting in the audience being nervous for you. And don't drop the diploma, it's bad luck!"

The two of them were sitting on her steps when he said, "I joined the Navy, Ellie."

"Joe!" she cried, her eyes wide and staring. "Oh, no, you couldn't! What do you mean, the Navy! Please say you're kidding, Joe. Please!"

"It was the best thing to do, Ellie. The very best thing."

Ellie leaned against him, but Joe made no move to touch her. "But, Joe. Oh, Joe—we planned, I mean everything is all set. And there's a war on and I don't want you to go to war."

Joe heard the brittleness in the girl's voice and knew

she was trying not to cry but he did not comfort her. "I'm not afraid of Viet Nam, Ellie. I'm afraid of here. I'm afraid for my brother."

"Paul's going to do okay, I just know it."

"Not Paul. Davey. I'm doing this for him, and maybe for me too."

"Davey?"

"Yes. Davey. As smart as Davey is, he won't be able to go to any college unless he gets a full scholarship. You understand—I mean a full one! There's money in the bank, but Momma doesn't think of it in terms of Davey, and Davey knows it. Yesterday I tricked Momma into going to Davey's school so she could sign for him to take part in a program that only nine kids in the whole city were picked for. They only wanted to talk to her, tell her what it was all about. But when she found out she wasn't looking for Paul, she left. She was right there, Ellie, right there *in* the school. All she had to do was walk down the hall. Once before, the school told Momma about Davey's ability and told her to encourage him, but she said something about she'd be glad if just one of her kids did the right thing. I had dropped out of school and I was beside her and she was trying to get her point over to me. And she dismissed what they were saying about Davey. Dismissed it! And Davey knew it. Just like I knew it. She didn't even mention what they said about Davey on the way home, for wondering where Paul was. And Paul wasn't messing with junk then."

"I'm sorry, Joe."

The boy put his arm around her then and pulled her close to him. One of the packages slipped down the steps a bit, but Joe didn't care. "Still want to marry me?" he asked softly.

"Yes, Joe."

"Why?"

She was crying now. "I don't know. But you and I were supposed to go to school together and get married in the college chapel, wearing African wedding clothes, and I was going to get pregnant the day we graduated. I mean, it was all planned, Joe, and you didn't have to join anything, you didn't."

"Sssh, Ellie, people are looking and your nose is getting snotty!" He laughed a little and hugged her tighter. "You know what?" he said. "I'll marry you. I'll double marry you!"

"Joe, please don't play."

"I'm not playing, Ellie," he said. "We'll get married and live in a magic place—where trouble never comes. In a teacup. A teacup full of roses."

"For real, Joe—will it come true?"

"Yes, if we believe it."

"I believe it."

"I believe it too," he said.

And by the time Joe started home, his packages coming apart, he did believe it.

When he got inside the house, Joe took his clothes out

of the boxes and bags and put them away. He hung his mother's dress on a hanger and took it in the kitchen and gave it to her. He winked at his father and aunt. "For you, Momma," he said. David was grinning.

Mattie turned the dress around and around, never smiling. "You know I don't wear no color like that," she said finally.

Joe saw the smile leave David's face and his mother looking for a price tag.

"When do I get a chance to wear a new dress? Don't nobody around here take me nowhere!" With that, she walked out of the kitchen with the dress and down the hall to her bedroom. Joe heard her open the closet door. Then she came out, put dinner on the dining-room table, and sat down to eat.

David began to eat but when he saw that his father and aunt were not eating, he stopped.

"You buy that dress for your mother to wear to your graduation?" Isaac Brooks said.

Mattie stopped eating.

"It's just a dress, Pop. She can wear it where she wants."

"It's not just a dress. Did you buy it so your mother could wear it to your graduation?"

"I told him I can't go 'cause I got to work. You know I make overtime every Thursday and Friday. Joe understands, so you got nothing to say." Joe noticed that his mother had lowered her voice. He waited. So did David and Aunt Lou.

"You didn't answer me, son. Was that dress for your mother to wear when you graduate tomorrow?"

"I wasn't sure whether or not she could make it, Pop," Joe said. "I just bought her a dress, that's all."

"She'll make it!" Isaac Brooks declared. His voice had some of its old strength.

David, his eyeglasses a little lopsided, looked at Joe.

"I already told them at work I was coming in," Mattie said.

"Take the dress back where you got it, Joseph," his father said, "and get your money."

"No, Pop."

"Then I'll take it back."

Aunt Lou was moving her head yes to something.

"Where'd you buy the dress, son?"

Joe didn't answer but he watched as his father got up from the table, went into the bedroom, came out with the dress, then went into Joe's room, got the correct box, put the dress in it, and laid the box on the buffet.

"I see your heart's not so sick, Brooks, you can't break bad. Nobody told him to buy nothing for me, though I'm glad he did. Goodness knows I need something!"

"That's right, I'm taking it back. Maybe somebody will come along and buy it for a woman who appreciates it. I remember once I gave my mother a pebble all wrapped up in a leaf. She held it in her hands and made over how nice a present it was and loved it!"

"You take that dress out here, Brooks—you better not come back!"

Again Joe noticed his mother's voice was lower than usual when she fussed. His father turned around and looked at her. He kept looking at her, his eyes hard and direct, his mouth steady, until the woman got up from the table, grabbed her plate, and slammed it down on the kitchen sink. She came back out of the kitchen. "Tell me I don't need the money, Brooks!"

"You don't need the money, Mattie!"

"Brooks, you are crazy."

"Take whatever you'd make doing overtime out the bank. Take it out of the part I put in!"

Mattie Brooks was speechless. Work out, Pop, Joe thought. Work out!

His mother was still staring.

"Or stay here and watch the house to keep Paul from robbing it clean, and I'll go! But one of us is going."

"Thank you, Jesus," Aunt Lou whispered. Joe heard her. "Thank you, Jesus!"

"I always worked two jobs, Mattie. You and the boys never been hungry and I can't even say that for myself. You never been cold in winter and I took you and the kids to beaches in the summer. But you were never satisfied. All you know is Paul."

"Oh, yeah, there you go! I knew you'd get around to Paul sooner or later!" Mattie's speechlessness was over. "Paul's great, you hear me!" she screamed. "Everybody knows that but you! He's got more talent, you understand, more talent than anybody you ever heard of, any time, any place and anywhere, black or white! It would

90

take fifty in my family and everybody in yours to make *one* Paul!" she yelled. "You hear me! You hear what I said!"

For a moment, her husband said nothing, just looked at his wife. When he spoke, his voice was almost a whisper. "You're sick, Mattie," he said. "And I regret the day I gave Paul life."

Mattie's mouth opened but she looked at Joe and David, and closed it. "How dare you, Brooks," she finally managed to murmur. "How dare you."

The father continued talking softly to her. "Joseph went out here and bought you something. Begging you, that's what he was doing, for something he shouldn't have to beg for."

Joe got up from the table.

"Sit down, Joseph," his father said. Joe did, and the man turned back to his wife again. "But what you did was throw it back in his face. I never seen no mother do nothing like that."

The dining room, with its tiny kitchen on one side and minute alcove on the other, was very still until Isaac Brooks pushed his plate away and opened up a newspaper. Joe knew his father usually took the plate to the kitchen and put it in the dishpan so 'Mattie don't have to carry it,' but he didn't do it this time.

Later that night, while his father watched television, Joe told him about joining the Navy and gave him the papers to sign.

"This what you really want?"

"Yes, Pop."

His father signed in all the places checked for his signature and gave the papers back to Joe. "Your mother loves you," he said, "and don't you forget it no matter where you go. Always write her. And I want you to talk to her as much as you can before you leave. There's a war on, you know. When you get over there, think about yourself first. Stay alive."

"I'm going to try, Pop."

"I think Mattie's coming to your graduation, but I won't make it. Except you know that even though I'm sitting here in the house I'll really be right there with you. I won't read the newspapers or watch television while I think you're up on that stage. I'm going to sit here and remember how proud of you I am."

"I know, Pop."

"I could make it to the graduation easy, but I got to stay here and watch for Paul. Once everybody's out this house, he'll steal it clean like he used to do before. Every time I went to the clinic and come back, something else was gone. I bought you a little toy juke-box phonograph when you were only ten and it was sort of like a thing we wanted to keep and maybe give to the grandchildren —but one day I come back and that was missing too. He's already taken a television out here, and he'll be itching for this one now that he's on that stuff again. But if he knows that I'm here, he'll lay off. He don't give me no off the wall, about nothing!"

When his mother signed the papers and gave them back to Joe, she put her arms around his neck and hugged him. "Brooks ain't taking that dress nowhere," she said.

Now, Joe thought, walking back to his own bedroom, it's time to talk to Davey.

9

"You must be a chump!"

"No, Joey," David said.

"Then how come you can't deal with money?"

"Because it's yours and I can't take it. You can stand there and make up all the stories and fairy tales you want."

"Davey, baby, I got no time for stories anymore, I'm leaving. You're on your own from now on and this is just a little to depend on. Something good. Something that works, when everything else lets you down."

"No, Joey."

"You got a big program coming up, Davey, and it's going to be a good year for you—but after that, what? What you got? It's time for college, a university or something. I know that's your thing!" Joe felt his calm slipping away. "Look, Davey," he said, "this money makes your dreams real, makes everything come true. Or at least it gets you started. It's a beginning. It keeps you from begging people, from asking. Also, I know you're going to need a winter coat, so this money means you got that coat already. You want to buy a book, buy a book. This money says you can. I don't care what you do with it. I'm leaving. Splitting. And it's going to be me and me alone for the next few years. I don't want to have to worry about nobody, most of all you."

Joe waited for David to say something, but his brother said nothing. His glasses, lopsided and low on his nose as usual, made him look goofy. It was a beautiful goofiness and Joe knew he'd remember his brother's look for a long time. He wished he could take David with him.

Joe turned around and opened the closet door. "Keep the money in this old jacket pocket. Paul won't look for it because he doesn't know anything about the money. Get it in the bank tomorrow, any bank you want. Here's my old bankbook in case some fool wants to know where you got it from. When you got the money in the bank under your own name —show my bankbook to the wind and let it blow." Joe shut the closet door and then he remembered the letter in his drawer. He opened the drawer and took it out. "Read this when you got some time," he said. "It's just some things I wanted you to know."

"But, Joey—"

"No, Davey, I don't hear you. Just do this for me and for you." Joe tucked the letter in the pocket with the money and shut the closet door again.

"I feel sorry for Paul, Joey."

"You ain't got the time to feel sorry for Paul. And don't lay none of this money on him. When he's talking money, don't listen. He goes from truth to lie to dream and back around again. Forget him."

"I thought he would go straight when he got out the hospital."

"I believed it too. But you and me ain't strong enough for Paul's needs. There's nothing you can do to make him come out of this. If he comes out, it's because he wants to."

"You really think he can't make it, Joey."

"I didn't say that. But whatever the reasons, Paul's trying hard to die. Maybe, if he's lucky, he will."

"I worry about Paul a lot, Joey. I don't want him to die."

"Neither do I, Davey," Joe said as he left the room. "I love the dude."

David sat on the bed and listened to his brother leave the house, then got up, went to the closet, got Joe's letter, and read it.

He read it two times before tears began to run down his face.

Outside, Joe felt good, and though it was late he called Ellie from a street phone. She couldn't talk but he didn't care, he still felt good. He called Phil but his mother said he was out.

Joe wished Willie were around. He felt like story time. Hannibal time.

"Hey, Brooky! How's your game running baby?"

Joe smiled at the voice. It came from a small black man with steel-gray eyes and a set of perfectly manicured, clear-polished fingernails.

Carolina Murphy.

A hustler's hustler. And a perfect person to move around with tonight, Joe thought, if Carolina let him. It depended on whether Carolina was out on business or just out.

Business was numbers. Some people said he had women on the payroll. Carolina hated the drug hustle and hated Warwick, Joe knew that. Everybody knew that. "I bring people good things," he had told Joe once, "stuff they can use." And another time he had said, "There ain't no bigger money than drug money. But I don't touch me no drugs."

10

_____

"You coming down all right, young stuff?"

"I'm coming down all right, Carolina," Joe said, and pointed to the car on the street. "You looking good, baby —that your new hog?"

"You like it, you can have it."

It didn't sound too unbelievable coming from Carolina, the way he said it. Carolina was like that. He could hang you up on a lie, just by the way he said it.

Joe looked again at the new-penny-colored Eldorado standing at the curb. He knew Carolina kept his cars, which he changed at a whim, clean inside and out. He was known to have the engines steam-cleaned two days in a row. Some hustlers dogged cars in order to keep up a certain image, but not Carolina. He kept his women and his clothes clean too.

He could almost make you believe his money was clean.

Carolina was wearing pea-soup-green knit slacks and a creamy-looking suede and knit matching top. His soft expensive leather shoes and his sheer nylon socks were also green.

"Your green is heavy, man," Joe said. "Where you heading?"

"Most likely jail."

Joe laughed.

"I get up each morning and dress for jail."

Joe laughed again. Being with Carolina could make you forget things. "Pop said the cops picked you up last week."

"He's right, they did. Cost me a few papers. Maybe they was going Christmas shopping early and needed some cash. A couple rookies trying out they hand, showing me who bigger. One had the nerve to yell at me, when I was leaving, 'Hey, Carolina!' Now, see, the only reason I let them say 'Carolina' without saying something back to them, something off the wall you understand, was 'cause they was black, see, and I'm trying to dig this brother thing. You know, they my brothers! So I turned around nice and looked at them. You know, a cultured, *nice* look. The youngest cat said, 'Where you going, Carolina?' And I cooled nice, said, 'To make back the money I just gave you.' "

Joe laughed hard.

"White cops say yes, Mister Murphy, and no, Mister Murphy—all the time they taking my money. But black cops don't give you no respect! Soon's they see me, they got to say 'Hey, Carolina,' like they done known me all my life. I said to one, I said, 'Mister, do I know you? I don't think I know you. But I must know you if you taking the liberty of familiar so much you got to yell Carolina like that. Here, you got to shake my hand. Now I know you! What's your name, baby?' "

Joe didn't think he'd ever stop laughing. But Carolina wasn't laughing at all.

"Same pay-offs, Brooky, same pay-offs. But the black cops don't handle it classy. They should watch white cops and see how it's done. There's a whole technique to stealing when you on the force. But it's like I always said. In some things, we just behind! Ain't no two sides about it."

Carolina always spoke as if he was dead serious, even when he was being funny.

"You still lying pretty well, Brooky?"

Joe's ears were beginning to ache from laughing so hard. "Yeah, I guess," he managed to say.

"The rate you make up a tale, I might can use you. You got a lot of heart, young stuff. Kids ain't got no heart no more. I used to get on down them dirt roads in South Carolina, and get it on. I wouldn't stop till I found me some people. Preferably, doing wrong."

Carolina walked over to the curb and opened the car door. He never locked it, but nobody would have touched it anyway. People said he had cameras rigged up inside, but Joe knew better. He had been in all Carolina's cars. It was just Carolina's attitude that made people think he had an edge on everything. Like the way he was sitting now, in the car.

"I got a short run to make," Carolina said. "Hop in and let's wheel. After that, I drop you home. The wrong people stop us, I don't know you—and you don't know me. If they say you was sitting in the car riding with me, tell them they lying!"

It was a together car, moving smooth, Joe thought.

"You look like you scared."

"Scared?"

"Yeah, like you scared to settle back. Go on and rest yourself—it might be years before I let you ride with me again. Turn on the tapes. Enjoy yourself. Carolina ain't gonna let nothing bad touch you."

Joe smiled, then shook his head and laughed.

"You don't sound so good laughing, Brooky. Sound better when you lying. Where we going now is a lie. People call it night life. Think they into something when they say that. They call it glamour, but I call it a lie. You checking that, you know what I mean?"

"Yeah, I think I know."

"The whole run is a lie, so what you say? And me— I'm a lie too. Tell Carolina you know what he talking about."

"I know what you talking."

"Good. Now you and me can wheel better together."

The "run" turned out to be a bar on a street narrow enough to be an alley.

At first it looked crowded, but Joe saw it was just the

way people were standing. Mostly around a pool table.

Lying on it was the biggest wad of money Joe had ever seen in his life. It looked almost like play money. It was real though. Real one-hundred-dollar bills.

But people paid more attention to Carolina's green outfit than to the green on the pool table. Joe kept hearing them say "You looking good, Carolina."

Carolina kept saying, "Got to, got to! Folks don't give you money when you wearing rags."

Later he explained it to Joe. "People don't part with cash if you ain't looking too tough. Wearing rags, going around cheap—makes them think ain't nobody else giving you nothing. That's bad for business. You got to look like money to get it. Remember that."

"I'll remember."

"Good. You want a drink, I'll get you a drink." Carolina pointed to an empty booth in back. "Sit there—you sit up front then you see too much," he said, walking over to the bar.

Joe's drink turned out to be a dressed-up Coke.

"They can't fix a decent drink for a kid no more. I been drinking all my life," Carolina said. "And I never seen no Coke served to nobody with two lemon slices and two cherries in it! They must been on sale this week, they got to give 'em away."

For a while, neither of them said anything, just watched the people. It was Joe who spoke first. "I joined the Navy today," he said.

"Good! You can make a lot of money in the service. I

learned in the Army—good training ground for perfecting hustles. I don't know about the Navy. When you come back, let me know."

"What kind of hustles?"

"You got to get on in there and see. My telling you ain't nothing, you understand. You got to get it your way." Carolina leaned against the dirty table. "But I tell you something. When I left, they wouldn't owe me nothing."

Joe would have laughed then but he knew Carolina wasn't joking.

"Work around, keep your eyes open, and see what you can do. Stay close to a sucker and when you see a in take it and do it good."

"Carolina?"

"Now I know you not going to ask me how!"

"No. This is something else."

"Carolina's listening."

"Keep an eye on Davey when I'm gone."

"Which goes along with what?"

"Just keeping an eye."

"I'll check him out here and there, if I ain't in jail. I live with that situation every day, you understand. But if I'm around, I'll watch him. You know that don't you, young folks?"

"Yeah. I know it, Carolina. Thanks."

"Just don't ask me to look out for Paul. I ain't got enough eyes for that."

"I tried to see Warwick, Monday, to talk about Paul.

But those clowns wouldn't let me near him. Warwick I mean."

Carolina put his drink down and took a long drag on his cigarette. "You got no business near Warwick. You can't deal with Warwick. Warwick will kick your behind. And if he don't, I will. Consider Warwick your enemy, or consider him dead, or what you want. But stay out his way."

Joe started to say something but Carolina's eyes stopped him.

"You can't touch Warwick. Forget him."

"I'm not afraid."

Carolina watched Joe for a long time. "How come you not scared. I'm out here dealing in the street all the time —and I'm scared! Everybody wants you. Your money and your behind. I always try to remember that. All my minutes is scared minutes. If I got to kill somebody, I'll do it. But that's scared time even more so, 'cause he might get me first."

Joe waited, and Carolina fell silent again. "Let me run it down to you," he finally said. "Warwick's money is top drawer and he ain't going to let a punk like you mess with it." There was no scorn in the word "punk" and Joe knew it. "I don't dig Warwick, but I admire his gold," Carolina said. "But I think he's stupid to keep a lot of grinning kids around him. I think he got problems— which ain't none of my business, you understand—but that part of his style I don't like, and the first time one of them punks says something to me, Warwick's going to be looking for somebody to fill that number spot. But they give me plenty room and I know I got to thank Warwick for that!"

"I wanted to talk to him about Paul. I was even going to do a few things for him, if he wanted, in a kind of exchange."

"You ain't too cool, Brooky baby. And I'm talking nice to you, 'cause I like you. But I'm thinking maybe you ain't too together."

"I'm together, Carolina."

"Okay. Then tell Carolina what you say to Warwick if he got near enough so's you could spit in his face. Tell Carolina what you say."

Joe couldn't answer. "I'd play it by ear," he finally said.

"Play your behind! And if Davey got ideas like that, I got no time for him."

"No, man."

"You sure?"

"I'm sure."

Carolina stood up. "I ain't got enough insurance to mess with kids. I keep an eye on Davey long as Davey keeps an eye on Davey."

"Thanks, Carolina."

"The minute he starts getting stupid, I don't owe you nothing."

Joe understood.

"Come on. Let's get you home."

"Hi, Carolina," a woman cooed when Joe and Carolina walked toward the door.

"I can't use it," Carolina told her. Moments later he slid matter-of-factly under the new-penny-colored steering wheel. "Always be careful what you use, Brooky. You know what I mean?"

"Yeah. I know what you mean."

The Cadillac pulled away from the curb. "Let's wheel," Carolina said in a make-believe high voice. "Let's wheel, babycakes!"

"I just might like the Navy," Joe said, watching streets and people move past them in a multicolored blend.

"Forget the Navy, Brooky—who taught you to drive?"

"You did, Carolina."

"What else Carolina do?"

"Like what?"

"What he tell you about liquor?"

"Drink the best."

"What he tell you about money?"

"Be greedy."

"What he say about women?"

Joe laughed. "Carolina, I just don't like big women, man!"

"Okay. Forget that, you change later. A whole lot of something good is better than a little bit something good —but what I tell you about cars?"

"No matter what you got, have a Cadillac too."

"Ain't this pretty thing getting you home good!"

"Yeah."

"I ain't even got to put my hands on the wheel!" Carolina Murphy took his hands off the wheel. "The Eldorado's something else, young stuff, baby. Damn if they can't *think!* Ain't it thinking? Look at it!"

"Yeah, Carolina, it thinks."

"Ain't it taking you home?"

"It's taking me home."

"What I say—keep yourself a big car and a big woman."

The house was dark when Joe got in. Everybody was sleeping. Except for Paul. He was sitting on a chair in the dark kitchen.

"I'm happy for you, little brother," he said. "Happy you graduating tomorrow."

"Today."

"Yeah. I always get mixed up on time, never know what time it is." For a moment he paused, then went on. "I came home wishing me and you could celebrate you graduating, only I ain't got no money and I don't look good enough to go nowhere. I'm sick and in a minute I'm leaving, 'cause I have to get straight. But I wanted to see you and talk to you first. I was sitting here remembering when I graduated."

Paul paused again, and Joe couldn't tell if it was because his brother felt pain or because he was thinking of what else to say.

"I walked all over," Paul continued, his voice ragged, "trying to get a job, a good job. Any good job—but it never came. There was nothing out there except mopping floors and washing dishes and carrying stuff up from basements. I wasn't against the work, I was against being forced to do it. At best, my hands were only an extra set of fingers for a nothing company." Paul stopped again and Joe knew it was because of pain. It was even stretching Paul's face. "I couldn't accept that," Paul whispered. "I wanted to collect blackness from my guts, my soul—and put it on paper, or cloth or walls or napkins or cardboard boxes or anything I could get my hands on." Paul stopped again. Sweat was beginning to appear on his face. He didn't seem to feel it. "Remember that art program they put me in in high school? That didn't help nothing come my way and every art school I looked into was a gyp. They couldn't guarantee me anything, not even a little promise—just took my money. I went in the Army and came out and the same things happened all over again. Remember?"

"I remember."

"I don't know if what I feel is good for you, but I want to give you some advice. Here it is. You tell nice stories, beautiful stories. But it's never going to help you for real, when you black—it'll just be something you can do. You'll see I'm right. Black talent, even black genius talent, may not get you nothing!"

"You wrong, Paul," Joe said. "I believe I can get what I want. I've always believed it. Like, maybe you could have set up a shop here in the house, man, and sold your stuff on the street, the corners, the bars, the schools. Anywhere, Paul. Black folks waiting for your stuff, but what you wanted was the super-star thing. You could have set your stuff up right outside this house and made it, man."

A violent pain seized Paul, for he stood up and walked, slightly bent, to the door. Another pain hit Paul but Joe reached him before he fell, helped him into a chair, grabbed paper towels, and wiped the perspiration from his face. "Stay with me, Paul. Fight the pain," Joe pleaded. "We can go down in the basement together and cold turkey. You and me. We won't come up till it's over and you're clean."

"No, little brother. I'm sick, man—I got to leave. I just wanted to see you and say a few things, but I can't think of half of it now. I stayed outside till all the lights went out before I came up, but when I looked in the room, you weren't there. So I waited." Paul's voice choked for a moment. "Get away from the door, I got to go."

"What about the basement, Paul?"

"I can't."

"Why don't you put a gun to your brain and blow it out all at once, Paul?"

Paul began to vomit. He wiped it on his sleeve. "You talking suicide and I can't do that, little brother—I'm too weak to hold the gun."

"Don't rush so, Joseph Matthew."

"Got to, Aunt Lou, I slept too late."

"Don't you rush, Joseph Matthew."

"Only way to move today. I got a lot to do—plus get my hair blown out and pick Ellie's gift up."

"Ellvira—Ellie coming tonight?" his father asked.

"Yeah, Pop," Joe said quickly, gulping coffee.

"Good," his father said, watching his sister sitting with her hands folded in her lap, staring.

"Isaac," she said when Joe walked out the door, "that child don't need to go nowhere near that school tonight. It ain't too clear to me yet, but I know."

Joe, his hair shaped and high, was pleased with the way Ellie's gift looked. The inscription he had had engraved on the eighteen-karat gold diploma charm read:

"ONCE UPON A TIME, THERE WAS A GIRL . . ."

JOE

Joe had the charm wrapped in the red, green, and black tri-colors of the Black Liberation flag. Black paper tied with green and red ribbons.

But that night after he finished dressing and helping David pick out what to wear, Joe moved the red and green ribbons on the small box to the side and pasted on a tiny teacup and roses he had cut from a magazine.

There was only one more thing he wanted to do.

11

"Do me a favor, Aunt Lou," Joe said. "Wear something bright and pretty to my graduation. Do it for me." Joe walked to her closet. "I want you to be the best-looking chick there. People will say 'Who's that lady over there looking so outasight!' " Joe was laughing. "And I'll say, 'Ain't nobody but my fine Aunt Lou!' "

His laughter stopped when he turned back and saw her. He wasn't prepared for her face.

It wasn't Aunt Lou's face; it seemed to belong to someone else.

He touched her. "Baby," he whispered, "Aunt Lou? You all right?"

Her body was rigid. Joe, because he didn't know what else to do, hugged her.

When she spoke, she was not talking to Joe. Her voice seemed very faraway. "This ain't got no reason. What they done, Lord Jesus, what they done? They ain't done nothing!"

Joe sat down on her bed and watched. He heard her mutter, "Joseph Matthew?"

"Yes, Aunt Lou?" Joe didn't know why he was whispering.

"Where you at?"

"Right here, Aunt Lou."

"Listen to me. You listening?"

"I'm listening, Aunt Lou."

"Don't you be scared, you hear me?"

"I'm not scared."

"Don't you worry, Joseph Matthew, 'cause it all going to be all right in the end—don't you worry."

The trance she was in held her body stiffly erect. Joe could see no sign of breathing in her thin chest, nor could he see her lips moving. Yet her words, seemingly suspended in air, were clear. Eyes staring, she had transcended the small close room with the old handmade wooden bed, the rough handmade muslin sheets.

"Joseph Matthew," she was saying, her words slipping out from somewhere. "Don't you be scared. You be strong. Tell me—is you strong?"

"I'm strong, Aunt Lou."

"I won't be resting in my grave if you forget the strength you got."

Joe was about to answer when he noticed her body relaxing and her face changing, softening. The rigid erectness was gone.

Aunt Lou was Aunt Lou again.

"You all right now?" Joe asked.

Aunt Lou looked at him sternly. "Joseph Matthew, why you sitting on my bed when you know I don't like nobody flopping down where I got to lay my head!"

This was Aunt Lou. Joe knew she was all right.

Joe went over to the closet and pulled out a light-tan crepe dress with flashing gray and beige beads around the neckline. "Here," he said, "wear this. I gave you this thing for Christmas last year and that's the last time you wore it—on Christmas day!" Joe laid the dress carefully across her bed. "Don't wear no black tonight."

"I got to wear what I got to wear, Joseph Matthew," she said in a too-quiet voice, but Joe didn't notice.

He kissed her. "I want to look up while this thing is happening to me and see you sitting there bright."

"I be with you, Joseph Matthew."

"That's good, Aunt Lou—you and me can celebrate my happy night."

Joe didn't hear her whisper softly, "No, Joseph Matthew, this ain't no happy night." And he had closed the bedroom door behind him when she reached for her good black dress. The one she wore to weddings and funerals.

"I guess I'm about ready to go, Pop."

Isaac Brooks got up and held his son as tight as he could. "Your mother's coming," he said. "She promised me."

Joe saw tears in his father's eyes for the first time in his life.

113

"You look good, Joseph. That beige suit laying on you perfect." Grasping Joe's hand tightly, his own hand was trembling. "Joseph," he said, wiping away his tears.

"Yes, Pop."

"I'm proud of you not just tonight but all the time. But you got to keep moving on. That's what makes you a man. It don't have nothing to do with schooling—it's deeper and harder than that, and you got to do it by yourself. You think you up to it?"

"Yes. Sir."

"That's what I want to hear. Now get on out here and do what you got to do and come on back and tell me about it. For your present from me and your mother, I'm giving you the same thing I gave Paul when he graduated. Your war bonds. The ones I bought specially for you ever since you were born. It'll be a nice piece of change." Isaac Brooks put his other hand on Joe's shoulder and drew him close again. When he let go, his eyes were dry. "Go on now," he said. "David and your Aunt Lou be along shortly."

Joe was on the last landing when he heard his aunt scream. The scream she called death.

12

The ceremony was a way of feeling and Joe felt it and felt good.

It was good to see David sitting there. Joe had expected to see a dumb grin on his brother's face but it wasn't there. Something was wrong on David's face. Joe tried to read it and couldn't. He tried to think of something else. I'm just sitting up here faking it, Davey. This kind of stuff is your stick, he thought.

Aunt Lou was there watching David. If she can't figure what's wrong, Joe thought, I sure as hell can't.

Ellie was there but her huge ponytail was gone. Her hair had been cut into a super-high and beautiful natural. Over and over, Joe saw the bright flashes of light from her camera. She stumbled once trying to take his picture.

Phil was there, sitting next to Ellie.

The only people missing are Pop and Momma and Paul, Joe thought. He could understand that but he couldn't understand David's face.

When the ceremony was over, noise and lights and excitement exploded over Joe and the other graduates.

Ellie got more pictures and a kiss which embarrassed her.

"Joe! You're not supposed to kiss like that in front of people!" she said, and handed him a small box wrapped in dark-brown satin. Inside was a poem in a miniature black-velvet frame:

> To Joe
> I
> wrote
> this
> poem
> to tell you
> of
> my love
> Ellie

Ellie had trouble opening Joe's present because she was sniffling and when she saw the diploma charm and read the inscription, she began to cry. Joe had to wipe her nose before he could open Phil's present.

"Ellie called me and told me about the Navy thing," Phil said, laughing. "So I figured you could use these."

When Joe opened the green box and saw the photographs he put the lid back on as fast as he could, grinning at Phil and looking quickly at Ellie and his aunt beside him.

But the old woman in the draped black dress said nothing, just hugged him.

Then David gave him a handmade cream-colored dashiki and pulled him aside.

Before David could say anything, Aunt Lou reached up and put her wrinkled fingers against his lips. David looked uncomfortable but he did not move.

Aunt Lou's face looked terrible.

She took her fingers away, and began to mumble. Joe thought she would scream, but she didn't and he was glad.

"Joey," David said.

It was then that Aunt Lou screamed. Ellie saw her twisted mouth and put her arms around her. Joe wanted to do something but he wasn't sure what. More important now was the way his brother looked.

"Davey, what's the matter? You been looking funny all night."

"Wait!" Aunt Lou was opening the little black pouch. "This got my whole life in it," she said, trembling.

Joe saw people beginning to gather around them. Then he heard David's voice.

"Paul found the money," David said. "The money's gone."

13

"He was coming here with me to see you graduate and he put on that old jacket to wear, where you hid the money. I tried to get him to wear something else, but by that time he had put his hand in the pocket and found it."

Joe felt as though he were enclosed in ice. Through it, he heard his aunt's voice.

"It done," she said.

Joe was still standing there when Phil started moving. "Let's go, baby," he said to Joe. "Maybe we can get him before he gives it up."

Joe came together quickly. "Davey," he said, half running behind Phil, who was moving fast toward the auditorium doors, "take Aunt Lou and Ellie home."

"Joe, I'm scared," Ellie cried. "Don't go!"

"That money's got a job to do, Ellie," Joe said.

David was running along beside Joe. "I'm going with you, Joey," he said.

"You can't handle this, Davey. Go home. Get Aunt Lou and Ellie out of here."

"I'm coming with you."

"*I said go home!*"

David was still there. Joe grabbed him and rammed him hard against an aisle seat. David stumbled backward. Someone was pulling Joe away but he held tight to David. "I said go *home!*"

Phil hollered, "We're losing time, baby."

Joe reached into his pocket, grabbed some money, and stuffed it into David's hand. "Go home!" he said and ran after Phil.

"You stay out of this, Phil," Joe said. "If I can't get Paul or if he ain't got it—I'm going all the way to Warwick. I'm getting Davey's money back."

"You got me with you then," Phil said. "What happens to you happens to me."

Phil saw Paul first. They both knew it was too late, but Joe searched Paul's pockets and socks and shirt and shoes anyway. The pants pockets were torn open.

The money was gone.

Joe grabbed his brother and slammed him against the frame of a metal doorway. "I ought to kill you," he cried. "Kill you!"

But Paul was in a deep nod. Somewhere where nobody but him could go.

Phil shook Paul violently. "Where's the money, man. Open them eyes and see me. Where's the money?"

119

But it was no use. Joe looked at his brother one more time. Then he walked away and didn't look back. If he had, he would have seen Paul lean all the way down and fall.

Joe and Phil were running again. Toward K Street this time. And Warwick.

"We need a gun," Phil said.

"No, Phil. All I want is Davey's money back."

"What we need is a gun," Phil said again.

"Then pretend we got one."

"O.K., but let's cool it, man," Phil said, "and walk. The cops see us, we get detained. They don't believe in black folks jogging."

They knew Warwick was in the K Street record shop when they saw his boys standing outside. The boys saw them coming and one left to go inside. "You see that, Phil—the fat one. The fat one's telling Warwick we here. I got a feeling the money's good."

"Your money's gone—we just here on principle."

"I think the money's good," Joe repeated.

"Been a long time since we rumbled, knocked some heads. How you feel? We getting close."

"Straight, Phil. I feel good."

"Then let's do it like we used to do it. Before we turned good and ruined ourselves."

Joe started grinning. "Phil," he said. "You ready?"

Phil grinned too and snapped his fingers. "Ready, baby. Just like the movies." Clowning with each other, they walked up to the eight boys leaning against the plate glass window. The fat one was back.

"Hey, Brooks," a boy near the end of the line called. "Somebody in your family musta hit the numbers!"

Joe's stomach felt cold. But the coldness was strength. He kept smiling when he spoke. "Which one you chicken monkeys going to tell Warwick I want to see him?"

Some of the boys laughed.

Quietly, and still smiling, Joe spoke again. "Let's see how good you are one at a time. I'll take the first four. Since it was my money and my brother. Then if you still can't get Warwick, Phil will take the other four. One-to-one. You use whatever you got on you. We use what we got on us."

There was silence.

"Who's first?"

Nobody moved.

"If this is the way I have to see Warwick, let it be."

One boy stepped out, or tried to. Joe's foot shot out swift and low, and the boy lay where he had fallen.

"*One!*" Phil yelled. His hand was under his jacket.

Joe fought two more before everything happened. He was fighting the third when another one jumped in and hit him. In a second Phil was beside him. Things were moving well when Joe heard Ellie screaming and police sirens. And David's voice.

"Davey! Get away! Get the hell out of here! I'll beat your ass if you don't get away from me!"

121

But David was doing all right. He was on top of the boy Joe'd been fighting, and Joe was proud of the way he was handling himself. He was moving in to help David when he heard the shot.

He turned and saw that two of Warwick's boys had guns. There were two more shots, and Joe saw the police taking cover.

But there was another boy with a gun, and he was not shooting wild. He was taking dead aim. At Joe. And there was no one near him, or near Joe.

Joe saw that it was the boy he had hit in the stomach the other day. "You mine, Brooks," he yelled.

Joe saw the cops moving in, and wondered, in a split second, if they could take the boy fast enough.

Joe was hit at the same time he heard the shot. The thing that hit him was David.

And the bullet hit David.

Joe leaped for the boy. Hit him, choked him, kicked him.

The policeman, who knew Joe and David, held back and let Joe do what he had to do. Except kill the boy.

Joe felt surrounded and he wanted to get away to his brother.

Ellie was there close. "Don't look, Joe," she cried. "Don't look."

14

Joe knelt down on the sidewalk beside his brother. He knew it was over. The wound had laid open the side of David's head.

Noise was everywhere, but Joe couldn't hear it. An ambulance siren was far off and coming closer, but he couldn't hear that either.

It didn't matter. He wasn't waiting for it. And neither was Davey.

Joe pulled his brother's jacket sleeve down a little. "Your arms are too long, Davey. They're always sticking out of things. But they come on right when you got a ball in your hand. Then, man, you got some pretty arms. Prettiest ones on a basketball court—anybody's court!

"But why you like to study so much? Night and day—just learning things. I could never get it easy as you could. I could get it a little, I guess. But not like you. Not easy." Joe smoothed his brother's collar. "Davey and the books."

The ambulance attendants were trying to put something over David's body but Joe wouldn't let them pull it over his face. "Can't you see I'm talking to him!"

The attendants moved away and Joe stretched out flat beside his brother and kissed him.

"Told you, Davey. People always doing wrong things, messing up. Even loving the wrong people. It wasn't a good place for you. You did everything too good. And that always means trouble." Joe leaned up and looked at David. "How you like Pop last night, Davey? Wasn't that something? He came on good, got hisself together. But I don't know about Momma and Paul. It's hard to tell about them."

Joe stretched out flat again and smiled. "Me? I'll make it, man. I'll make it for you—I promise you, Davey. Wherever I go, you'll be there too. When I do good things, you be doing them with me. In fact, if I do good at all— it'll be 'cause you there with me, man. Yeah, I know it sounds simple, but that's the way it's going to be."

Joe turned away from his brother for a moment to look at Ellie kneeling on the ground beside him. He turned back to David. "When Ellie and me get married and have some kids, I'm going to name my tallest and smartest son after you. I won't name none of them until they all get here and I can figure out which one that is."

Joe started crying. Then he stopped, and put his face against David. "Hey, Davey," Joe said, his voice barely a whisper. "Hey, man—let me tell you 'bout a place." Joe tried to get his face even closer to his brother's, and Ellie, watching him, moved closer to Joe. "Yeah," Joe was saying, "I know. I know you don't dig my stories no more 'cause you think you too big—but you going to hear this one."

Ellie put her hand on Joe's trembling shoulder. He was crying hard.

"You'll like it, man. Everything is real good there, Davey—good like you. Nobody got to worry and fight and stuff like that. The people are together, and trouble never comes. All the mothers love you and tell you, Davey. I swear, man. And all the fathers are strong. The sisters are pretty. And the brothers help each other. It's a love place. A real black love place." Joe tried to smile and couldn't. "I wouldn't kid you, Davey. Only the smart ones get to go—people like you. The good ones."

Joe felt like he was choking. Some giant thing was closing his throat. He reached for Ellie's hand and held it tight. Then he lay closer to his brother's body and hugged it hard. He kissed David's face and tried to hold it, made a fist and brought it gently to his brother's face. Then he reached back and pulled the heavy white cover, put it lightly over David's face. Strong hands were coming from somewhere now, pulling him up. But Joe held tight to David, buried his face on his brother's chest. He didn't know he was yelling.

"Good luck, Davey," he cried. "Good luck, man."